Guardians of the Island

Published by Amazon UK.
Edited by Sarah Hughoo and Susan Elliott.
Cover design by Paul Seager.

This book is a work of fiction. Any resemblance to actual persons, living or dead, events, or locales is entirely coincidental.

For information, contact:
Amazon UK Publishing

First Edition: 2024

ISBN: 9798308514602

Printed in the United Kingdom

Foreword

In a world filled with uncertainty, the strength of community shines brightest in times of adversity. **Guardians of Kos** is a tale woven from the threads of resilience, unity, and the indomitable human spirit. It tells the story of a retired special forces operator who finds peace on a tranquil Greek island, only to confront the shadows of his past and a formidable enemy determined to seize control.

As you journey through these pages, you'll witness the power of collaboration and the unwavering bonds that can form when individuals come together for a common cause. This story is not just about fighting against an external threat; it's about the personal battles we all face and the courage it takes to confront them. Join Kurt and the villagers of Kos as they embrace their destiny and fight to protect what truly matters.

Dedication

For the brave souls who have fought for freedom and for those who continue to stand together in the face of adversity. May we always find strength in our communities and solace in our shared stories.

Chapter 1:

The Hermit's Life

Kurt stood at the edge of his modest terrace, overlooking the azure expanse of the Aegean Sea, the sunlight casting shimmering diamonds on the water's surface. The island of Kos was a world away from the chaos he once knew—a sanctuary nestled among the rugged hills and craggy cliffs. His days had settled into a comfortable rhythm, one that offered solitude and a reprieve from the ghosts of his past.

Every morning, he rose with the sun, its golden rays creeping over the mountains like a gentle hand. He'd brew a strong cup of Greek coffee, the aroma rich and inviting, and savor it while watching the world wake up.

After breakfast, he would strap on his well-worn boots, lace them tightly, and set off on the winding path that led to the summit where the old church stood.

The climb was a daily ritual, a pilgrimage of sorts. Each step was a meditation, the rhythm of his breath syncing with the heartbeat of the mountain. The air was crisp, carrying the scent of wild thyme and sage, while the chirping of cicadas serenaded his ascent. Kurt welcomed the solitude; it allowed him to escape the memories that often lingered like shadows, threatening to consume him.

As he reached the church, a small stone structure adorned with simple whitewashed walls and a blue dome, he took a moment to appreciate its beauty. It had become a place of solace for him, a testament to his newfound life. Here, he tended to the flowers that surrounded the building, their vibrant colors a stark contrast to the starkness of his former existence. He would sweep the steps, light candles, and reflect on his journey, allowing his thoughts to drift freely.

His afternoons were spent exploring the island, sampling the local cuisine at a taverna in the village below. The laughter of fishermen and the clinking of wine glasses filled the air as he enjoyed dishes of grilled octopus, moussaka, and a glass of robust red wine. The tavern owner, an old man named Nikos, had become a friend, sharing stories of the island's history while Kurt listened, half lost in the tales and half in his own thoughts.

Though life here was serene, Kurt's past was never far from the surface. Flashbacks would invade his tranquility, memories of missions gone awry and the treachery he had witnessed during his years in the SAS. Faces would haunt him—those of comrades lost and enemies vanquished. He would often find himself staring out at the horizon, grappling with the weight of what he had done, questioning whether he truly deserved this peace.

On this particular day, as he descended the mountain, the sun began to dip toward the horizon, painting the sky in hues of orange and purple. He was lost in thought, contemplating the simplicity of his life, when he noticed movement up ahead. A group of tourists had ventured onto the trail, their laughter echoing through the serene landscape. He smiled faintly, amused by their carefree energy, a stark contrast to his solitary existence.

But then his heart sank. Among them was a face he recognized, a face he had thought was lost to the past—a ghost from a life he had desperately tried to leave behind. The moment their eyes locked, a jolt of recognition shot through him. This was no ordinary tourist; this was one of the treacherous figures from his past, a man he had thought dead—a man he had sworn to eliminate.

Kurt's instincts kicked in, a mix of adrenaline and dread coursing through him. He felt the familiar rush of danger creeping in, shattering the peace he had built. The serene beauty of

Kos faded, replaced by the harsh reality of his former life. He was no longer a hermit enjoying the sunlight; he was a target, and the hunter had become the hunted.

Chapter 2:

A Ghost from the Past

Kurt's heart raced as he stepped back into the shadows of the trees lining the trail. The laughter of the tourists faded into an echo, but the weight of recognition hung heavily in the air. His mind was a whirlwind of thoughts, churning memories that he had tried so hard to bury.

The man among the tourists was Viktor Grigori, a former operative in a shadowy network that Kurt had battled years ago. He was a ruthless trader in human lives, his escape from justice an open wound in Kurt's psyche. They had crossed paths once, during a covert operation in Eastern Europe that had gone tragically wrong. Kurt had thought he'd ended Viktor's reign of terror, a final act of justice after weeks of chasing the elusive target. But here he was, alive and smiling, completely oblivious to the storm brewing in Kurt's mind.

Kurt pressed his back against the rough bark of a tree, his breath steadying as he fought the urge to confront the ghost of his past. Instead, he closed his eyes, attempting to recall the details of that fateful encounter. It was a cold night in Bucharest when everything had fallen apart. They had exchanged gunfire in a dilapidated warehouse, the air thick with smoke and the cries of the desperate. Kurt had been forced to make a choice—one that had cost lives.

Viktor's cunning had allowed him to slip away, his escape a painful reminder of Kurt's failure. The thought of facing him now, in this tranquil paradise, felt like a cruel twist of fate. The peace he had carved out for himself seemed a mockery of the chaos that had just resurfaced.

As he crouched there, memories flooded back. He remembered the grim faces of his fallen comrades, the haunting looks of those he couldn't save. The weight of responsibility sat heavily on his shoulders, each loss a ghost that refused to fade. Kurt had built his life on the hope that he could atone for those mistakes, that he could live in harmony with the world. Now, it seemed, the world had other plans.

With a newfound resolve, he decided to keep his distance. Observing Viktor from afar was the safer choice—one that would allow him to gather information without drawing attention to himself. He shifted his position slightly, peering through the leaves as the group passed by, Viktor leading them with a swagger that Kurt once would have admired.

The tourists chatted animatedly, their joy a stark contrast to the turmoil swirling in Kurt's gut. As they approached, he caught snippets of their conversation—Viktor sharing tales of adventure, embellishing his past, perhaps even hinting at a darker side that Kurt knew all too well. The tourists listened, rapt, oblivious to the danger lurking in their midst.

Kurt felt a flicker of anger. How could they be so naive? Did they not sense the predatory energy radiating from him? For Kurt, the laughter felt like a distant memory, a reminder of what he had sacrificed for a life filled with blood and betrayal. He clenched his fists, every muscle in his body tensing with the urge to protect those unaware of the threat.

Just then, Viktor turned slightly, his gaze sweeping over the area. Kurt froze, his heart pounding in his chest. They locked eyes for the briefest moment, and time seemed to slow. Viktor's smile faded, replaced by a glimmer of recognition. Kurt's instincts screamed at him to retreat, but he remained rooted in place, a shadow in the fading light.

"Something wrong?" one of the tourists asked, glancing at Viktor, who shook his head, dismissing the concern.

Kurt's breath hitched as he backed further into the thicket. He couldn't let his past consume him; he needed a plan. With a quick glance at the retreating group, he turned on his heel and started back up the mountain, each step heavy with the weight of the confrontation he was trying to avoid.

As he climbed higher, his mind raced with thoughts of Viktor's potential motives. What had brought him to Kos? Was he merely a tourist, or was there something more sinister at play? Kurt could feel the tension tightening around him like a noose, a reminder that his old life was not done with him yet.

When he reached the church, the peaceful ambiance of the place felt tainted. The flickering candles and vibrant flowers seemed to mock his turmoil. He sank onto a weathered bench outside, the stones cool beneath him. The sounds of the island faded, replaced by the haunting echoes of gunfire and cries for help.

Kurt closed his eyes, forcing himself to breathe deeply. He had trained for this—trained to handle fear, to remain composed under pressure. But nothing could prepare him for the emotional storm that had just erupted within him.

In that moment of solitude, he knew that he could not allow Viktor to dictate his life any longer. He had fought for his peace, and he would not let a ghost from his past rob him of it. He needed to confront Viktor, not with violence, but with the knowledge that he had moved beyond the shadows of his former self.

With resolve settling in his heart, Kurt stood up, looking toward the path leading back down. He was determined to learn more about what Viktor was planning, to unravel the threads of this new threat before it ensnared him once again. The sun dipped lower on the horizon, casting long shadows across the land, but Kurt felt a flicker of light igniting within him—a spark of defiance.

Chapter 3:

Unravelling Tension

Kurt's mind raced as he descended from the church, his heart pounding with the urgency of the moment. He navigated the narrow, winding paths that crisscrossed Kos, his thoughts a tempest of strategies and contingencies. The island that had once felt like a sanctuary now brimmed with the potential for chaos. He could not allow Viktor to disrupt the fragile peace he had painstakingly built.

As he reached the village, the sounds of laughter and music spilled into the streets, a stark contrast to the storm brewing within him.

He paused outside Nikos' taverna, the familiar aromas of grilled meats and fresh bread wafting through the air, but he had no appetite for comfort. Instead, he needed information anything that could give him insight into Viktor's intentions.

Kurt stepped inside, the warm glow of the tavern enveloping him. Nikos was behind the bar, chatting with a few locals, his jovial demeanor an unyielding force against the backdrop of Kurt's anxiety. The old man noticed him and waved, his smile brightening the room.

"Kurt! Come, join us! You must try the new dish!" Nikos called, his voice booming with good-natured enthusiasm.

Kurt forced a smile, but his mind was elsewhere. "Not today, Nikos. I need to ask you something."

The tavern owner's expression shifted, concern etching lines across his face. "Of course. What troubles you?"

Kurt leaned in closer, lowering his voice. "Have you seen any unusual tourists lately? Anyone that stands out?"

Nikos frowned, considering the question. "Unusual? This is a tourist island. Everyone comes for the sun and the sea." He glanced around, then lowered his voice. "But I did hear whispers about a group coming in, some men who seem... more interested in the island than just relaxation."

Kurt's interest piqued. "What do you mean?"

"They speak in hushed tones, gathering at night. I overheard them mentioning business, but not the kind you'd find in a tavern." Nikos glanced around again, ensuring no one else was listening. "They don't seem like your average holidaymakers."

Kurt's gut twisted. "Do you know where they're staying?"

Nikos nodded, his brows knitted in concern. "At the old hotel by the coast. But be careful, Kurt. These men do not seem friendly."

"Thank you, Nikos," Kurt said, determination flooding his veins. He stepped back into the street, the sun now dipping below the horizon, casting an orange glow over the village. The shadows lengthened, mirroring the darkness creeping into his thoughts.

As he walked, Kurt's instincts kicked into overdrive. He needed to gather information on Viktor and the group he had aligned himself with. There was no room for hesitation; he was in a race against time.

He made his way toward the coast, the sound of waves crashing against the rocks echoing in the distance. The old hotel loomed ahead, a relic from a bygone era, its faded elegance a stark reminder of the island's storied past. He approached the entrance, his senses heightened, scanning for any sign of Viktor or his associates.

The lobby was empty, the dim lighting casting an eerie atmosphere. Kurt slipped into a corner, using the shadows to his advantage. He listened closely, hoping to catch a snippet of conversation that might provide the intel he needed.

Moments passed, and just as doubt began to creep in, he heard footsteps approaching. Two men entered, their voices low but urgent. Kurt's heart quickened as he strained to hear their conversation.

"...everything is in place. He has no idea what's coming," one of the men said, his tone laced with malice.

"Good. We need to act quickly. If he figures it out, we'll lose the opportunity," replied the second man.

Kurt's blood ran cold. They were planning something, and he had to find out what it was. He leaned in closer, the tension in the air palpable as they moved toward a small table in the corner.

"Is Viktor ready?" the first man asked, glancing around to ensure they were not overheard.

"Of course. He's been waiting for this moment for years," the second replied. "It's time for him to settle the score."

Kurt's mind raced. They were not just here for a holiday; they had a mission, and he was at the center of it. He needed to warn Nikos, to protect the innocent tourists who had unwittingly wandered into the crossfire.

Just then, one of the men turned, and Kurt froze. The last thing he needed was to be seen. He ducked behind a potted plant, his heart pounding as he watched the men, their eyes scanning the lobby as if sensing something amiss.

Kurt's thoughts shifted into high gear. He had to find a way to disrupt their plans, but how? He couldn't take them all on alone, especially without risking further violence in a place he had come to love.

He considered his options. Gathering information was crucial, but so was formulating a plan that would allow him to act without drawing attention to himself.

As the men settled at their table, Kurt made a swift decision. He would tail them, find out where they went, and then return to Nikos to strategize. It was a dangerous gamble, but he had no other choice. The shadows were closing in, and he needed to stay one step ahead.

Quietly, he slipped out of the hotel, blending into the night as he followed the men down the cobbled streets. The thrill of the chase ignited a familiar spark within him—a reminder of the life he had left behind, but this time, he was determined to rewrite the ending.

Chapter 4:

The Confrontation

Kurt moved through the labyrinthine streets of Kos with purpose, his instincts sharpened by adrenaline. The two men he followed seemed to have no inkling they were being trailed. They walked with an air of confidence, their conversation punctuated by quiet laughter that felt out of place against the backdrop of Kurt's growing tension.

As they approached the harbor, the scent of saltwater filled the air, mingling with the sounds of the night—distant music from the taverns and the soft lapping of waves against the docks. The moon hung low in the sky, casting a silver glow that illuminated their path.

Kurt kept a safe distance, staying in the shadows. The men paused at a secluded dock, where a sleek black boat bobbed gently in the water. It was a striking contrast to the quaint fishing boats lining the harbor, its presence a warning sign of the trouble lurking beneath the surface.

"Is he coming?" one of the men asked, glancing back toward the village, his expression tense.

"Viktor said he would be here. Just keep your eyes open," the other replied, scanning the area with a predatory gaze.

Kurt's heart raced as he considered his next move. He needed to get closer, to hear everything. The stakes were too high to risk missing any vital information. He crouched behind a stack of crates, the rough wood digging into his knees, and waited for the right moment to approach.

Minutes passed, each tick of time amplifying the unease building in his chest. Just when he thought he might have to make his presence known, a figure emerged from the shadows. It was Viktor, striding with the same confidence Kurt had seen earlier, but now there was an intensity in his eyes that sent a chill down Kurt's spine.

"Let's not waste time," Viktor said, his voice low but commanding. "We have a job to do, and it's best done under the cover of darkness."

Kurt's breath caught in his throat. This was it. Whatever plan they had was about to unfold, and he couldn't afford to be on the sidelines any longer. He had to confront Viktor and put an end to this before it escalated into violence.

Steeling himself, Kurt crept closer, ensuring he was just out of sight while still within earshot. The tension in the air was thick, a palpable energy crackling like static.

Viktor leaned in closer to his companions, speaking in hushed tones. "We're going to lure him in, make him think he's safe. He won't see it coming until it's too late."

Kurt's blood boiled at the implications. They were planning a trap, one that could ensnare not just him, but innocent people who had no idea of the danger lurking beneath the surface.

He weighed his options quickly. Confronting Viktor directly could lead to chaos, but doing nothing was not an option. He needed to act, to disrupt their plan without revealing himself.

With a surge of determination, he picked up a loose rock and tossed it toward the opposite side of the dock, creating a soft splash in the water. The sound echoed in the stillness of the night, drawing the attention of the men.

"What was that?" one of them hissed, turning sharply.

Kurt seized the moment. He slipped around the crates, moving quickly yet quietly, positioning himself within earshot but hidden from view. He could feel his pulse quicken as he readied himself for what was to come.

Viktor turned his head slightly, narrowing his eyes. "Stay sharp. We can't afford any mistakes now."

The three men huddled closer, and Kurt's heart raced as he focused on their exchange, adrenaline sharpening his senses. He could hear every word, every shift of their bodies.

"Once we have him, we'll make him pay for everything he took from us," Viktor declared, his voice dripping with venom. "He'll wish he'd never come back."

Kurt's jaw clenched, fury igniting within him. He stepped out of the shadows, emerging into the dim light of the moonlit dock. "You think I'm just going to let you do that?"

Viktor and his companions turned in shock, eyes widening in disbelief. Kurt stood his ground, his presence a stark contrast to the trio. He had spent too long hiding from his past; now it was time to confront it head-on.

"Kurt…" Viktor's expression shifted from surprise to a twisted grin. "I was wondering when you'd show up. I was beginning to think you'd lost your edge."

Kurt's fists tightened. "You've overstayed your welcome, Viktor. Whatever plans you have, they end here."

Viktor chuckled, an unsettling sound that sent a shiver down Kurt's spine. "You think you can intimidate me? You're just a washed-up soldier playing at being a hermit. But I see you're still the same man beneath it all—ready for a fight."

The tension crackled like lightning in the air. Kurt's muscles coiled, ready for action. "I'm not playing games anymore. Leave this island, or you'll find out how dangerous I can be."

Viktor stepped forward, his demeanor shifting from playful to predatory. "You really believe you can stop me? You don't understand the stakes here."

Kurt's voice was steady, fueled by years of training and the weight of his past. "Try me."

With that, Viktor lunged, and the fight erupted. Kurt reacted instinctively, his body moving as if it had been trained for this moment. He sidestepped Viktor's attack, using the momentum to deliver a swift kick that sent him staggering back.

The other two men sprang into action, but Kurt was ready. He ducked and rolled, evading their blows while leveraging his surroundings. The fight transformed the tranquil dock into a chaotic battlefield, the sound of fists hitting flesh and grunts of exertion filling the air.

Kurt fought with precision, utilizing the skills honed during years of service. He could feel the rush of adrenaline fueling him, but this was different; it was more than just a fight—it was a reckoning.

Viktor recovered quickly, lunging at Kurt again, his fury palpable. The two clashed, grappling as they fought for dominance. Each punch exchanged echoed the history between them, a culmination of pain, betrayal, and unresolved conflict.

Kurt's mind raced, recalling every detail from their past encounters, every lesson learned on the battlefield. He pushed through the fatigue, his focus unwavering.

"Why are you really here, Viktor?" Kurt shouted, trying to gain the upper hand. "What do you want?"

Viktor grinned, a manic light dancing in his eyes. "Revenge, of course. You left me for dead. I'm here to finish what we started."

With a surge of strength, Kurt broke free from Viktor's grip, delivering a solid blow to his gut. As Viktor doubled over, gasping for breath, Kurt took a moment to assess the situation.

The other two men were regrouping, preparing to charge again. Kurt knew he had to end this quickly. He took a deep breath, grounding himself as he prepared to face them head-on.

"Enough games," he declared, his voice steady and commanding. "You want me? Then let's finish this."

The three men closed in, but Kurt stood his ground, ready to confront his past once and for all.

Chapter 5:

Memories and Regrets

The chaos of the fight surged around him, the adrenaline coursing through Kurt's veins, heightening every sense. He stood poised, muscles tense, ready for the next move. Viktor's two companions advanced, eyes glinting with malice. Kurt could see their intentions clearly—this was not just a fight; it was a reckoning, a culmination of years of buried memories and unhealed wounds.

As they closed in, Kurt's mind flashed back to the day it all began. The mission that had changed everything. He remembered the cold steel of his weapon, the adrenaline surging as he prepared to breach the enemy stronghold. He had been confident, surrounded by comrades he trusted with his life. But that confidence had been misplaced.

The operation in Bucharest had been planned meticulously, but as they moved in, everything spiraled out of control. The ambush had been sudden and brutal. Kurt had fought fiercely, his training kicking in as chaos erupted around him. Gunfire echoed, and explosions rocked the ground beneath their feet. In the confusion, he had lost track of Viktor, the target he was sworn to eliminate.

Kurt's breathing quickened as the memories flooded back. He had cornered Viktor in that derelict warehouse, adrenaline pumping through his body. Just as he was about to pull the trigger, a shot rang out from behind—a comrade's cry cut through the din, drawing his attention away. In that split second of distraction, Viktor had slipped through his fingers, vanishing into the shadows while Kurt was left to face the consequences of that moment.

"Keep your focus!" his commanding officer had shouted as they regrouped. "We can't lose anyone else!"

But they had lost so much that night—lives, trust, and a part of Kurt that he would never reclaim. The weight of that mission had haunted him ever since, a specter lurking just beneath the surface of his newfound life on Kos. Now, facing Viktor once more, the ghosts of the past threatened to consume him.

Kurt shook his head, forcing himself back to the present. The two men charged at him, their eyes filled with fury. He dodged the first blow, countering with a swift kick that sent one of them crashing into the edge of the dock. The other lunged at him, and Kurt met him head-on, grappling for control.

"You think you can win this?" the man spat, struggling against Kurt's grip. "You're outnumbered!"

Kurt tightened his hold, memories still swirling in his mind. "I've faced worse odds," he replied, channelling the strength of his past. "And I've always come out on top."

With a surge of power, he threw the man to the ground, using his momentum to pivot and face Viktor. The time for hesitation was over; the confrontation was at hand.

Viktor had recovered, his eyes burning with a twisted sense of vengeance. "You should have stayed hidden, Kurt. You think your little life here can protect you from me?"

Kurt felt a mix of anger and determination rise within him. "I'm not afraid of you. Not anymore."

The two men squared off, the tension thick in the air. Kurt could feel the past pressing in on him, the weight of his failures, but he also felt the strength of his resolve. He wouldn't let Viktor's presence dictate his fate any longer.

With a fierce battle cry, they lunged at each other, the clash of fists echoing in the night. The fight was brutal, each blow fueled by years of resentment and regret. Kurt recalled every moment from that night in Bucharest, the lives lost, the mistakes made, and the determination to make things right.

As they fought, Kurt's mind flitted back to his comrades—men who had stood by him, fought with him, and ultimately paid the price for his choices. He could see their faces, hear their laughter, and feel the camaraderie that had once defined his life. Each memory added fuel to his fire, a reminder of what was at stake.

Viktor landed a punch to Kurt's side, the impact jolting him. Pain shot through him, but he pushed it aside, using the adrenaline to fuel his next move. He countered swiftly, catching Viktor off guard with a well-timed jab to the jaw, sending him staggering back.

"Why do you want to drag this out?" Kurt demanded, breathing heavily, sweat trickling down his forehead. "You lost. Accept it."

Viktor wiped the blood from his mouth, a malevolent grin spreading across his face. "I'm not the one who lost, Kurt. You are. You think this is about revenge? This is about power. You took something from me, and now I'm going to take everything from you."

In that moment, everything clicked into place for Kurt. Viktor wasn't just here for revenge; he was trying to regain control over a life that had spiraled out of his reach. Kurt realized he wasn't just fighting for his own survival; he was fighting for those who had fallen, for the men who could never fight again.

With renewed strength, Kurt charged at Viktor, channelling his memories into one final, decisive blow. The collision reverberated through the dock as Kurt's fist connected with Viktor's face, a release of pent-up rage and regret.

Viktor stumbled back, crashing into the side of the boat. Kurt stood over him, breathing heavily, the echoes of his past ringing in his ears. "You're done, Viktor. This ends now."

As Viktor looked up at him, the defiance in his eyes began to fade, replaced by a flicker of fear. Kurt had finally turned the tide, reclaiming the power he thought he had lost.

But before Kurt could relish the moment, he heard footsteps approaching from behind. The two men who had fought alongside Viktor were regaining their footing, ready to charge once more.

Kurt's mind raced. He needed to end this confrontation, but he couldn't let the others overpower him. He glanced around, searching for a way out.

"Viktor," he said, his voice steady but urgent. "If you want to live, you need to leave. Now. I won't hesitate to finish this."

The tension hung in the air, thick and heavy. For a moment, it seemed as though the world had frozen, waiting for Viktor's response.

Finally, Viktor let out a low chuckle, but there was no humor in it—only a dark undertone. "You think you can scare me? You have no idea what I'm capable of."

Kurt's resolve hardened. He wasn't afraid of Viktor; he was afraid of what Viktor might do if given the chance to escape.

"Leave," Kurt demanded again, his voice low and commanding.

Viktor's expression shifted as he realized the precariousness of his position. He looked at his companions, who were still recovering, and then back at Kurt.

"Fine," he spat, his tone laced with venom. "But this isn't over, Kurt. You've only delayed the inevitable."

With a final glare, Viktor turned and fled down the dock, the other two men hesitating for a split second before following. Kurt watched them vanish into the shadows, the weight of the confrontation still heavy on his shoulders.

As silence enveloped the dock, Kurt felt a mix of relief and lingering tension. He had confronted Viktor, but the threat wasn't entirely gone. The past had come roaring back to life, and he knew that this would not be the last time they crossed paths.

With the adrenaline slowly fading, Kurt took a deep breath, grounding himself in the present. He had survived, but at what cost? The memories of his comrades weighed heavily on his heart, a reminder of the sacrifices made.

He knew he had to be vigilant; the shadows of the past were far from extinguished. As he left the dock, determination coursed through him. He would not let Viktor's presence steal his peace again. This was just the beginning.

Chapter 6:

The First Move

Kurt emerged from the shadows of the dock, his heart still racing from the confrontation. The cool night air brushed against his skin, a stark contrast to the heat of the fight. He needed to regain his composure and formulate a plan; this battle was far from over.

As he made his way back through the winding streets of Kos, his mind whirred with possibilities. Viktor's escape didn't just represent a threat to Kurt—it posed a danger to the very fabric of the island he had come to cherish. The peaceful life he had built was now at risk, and he wouldn't let that happen.

Kurt arrived at his small cottage, a simple structure nestled among the olive trees. He flicked on a lamp, the warm glow casting a comforting light across the modest room filled with mementos of his life on the island. He took a moment to breathe deeply, grounding himself in the familiar surroundings. This was his sanctuary, a place where he had found solace from the chaos of his past.

He moved to the small table in the corner, spreading out a map of Kos. His finger traced the coastline, lingering on the location of the old hotel where Viktor and his companions had gathered. He needed to gather more information—find out what they were planning and how he could disrupt their operations.

But first, he needed allies. He couldn't confront Viktor alone; he needed to reach out to someone he could trust. He thought of

Nikos, the tavern owner who had shown him kindness since he'd arrived on the island. Nikos was well-connected and knew the ins and outs of the village. He could be a valuable resource in Kurt's quest for information.

Kurt grabbed his jacket, slipping it on as he stepped outside, the moonlight illuminating the path before him. He walked briskly through the village, determined to reach Nikos before the night deepened. The sounds of the tavern grew louder as he approached, the laughter and music spilling out into the street.

As he entered, the warm atmosphere enveloped him. Nikos was behind the bar, serving drinks to a handful of locals. His jovial demeanor brightened the room, a stark contrast to Kurt's brooding thoughts.

"Kurt! You've returned! Join us!" Nikos called, waving him over.

Kurt smiled but waved it off. "I need to talk to you, Nikos. It's urgent."

The tavern owner's expression shifted to one of concern as he wiped his hands on a towel. "Of course. What troubles you?"

Kurt leaned in, lowering his voice. "I need information about some tourists staying at the old hotel. They're not who they seem."

Nikos raised an eyebrow, his interest piqued. "What do you mean?"

Kurt glanced around to ensure no one was listening. "There's a man named Viktor. He's dangerous, and I believe he's plotting something."

The old man's brow furrowed, his demeanor turning serious. "Viktor? I've heard whispers about him. What is he planning?"

"I don't know the specifics, but he has associates with him, and they seem to be involved in something illicit. I need your help to find out more," Kurt explained, urgency lacing his words.

Nikos nodded, his expression contemplative. "I have my ear to the ground. I can help, but you must be careful. If they catch wind of your inquiries, it could put you in danger."

Kurt appreciated Nikos's concern but knew he couldn't back down now. "I'll be careful. I just need information about their movements—who they meet, what they're doing. Any little detail could help."

Nikos contemplated for a moment before nodding. "I can ask around. I'll speak to some of my contacts tonight. But you must promise me you won't take unnecessary risks."

"I promise," Kurt replied, his resolve firm. "I'm done hiding."

As they spoke, the tavern door swung open, and a figure stepped inside. Kurt's breath hitched as he recognized the newcomer—a man from Viktor's group. He wore a dark leather jacket and surveyed the room with an air of confidence that instantly put Kurt on high alert.

"Nikos!" the man called, striding toward the bar. "I need a drink."

Kurt's instincts flared. He quickly ducked behind a nearby table, watching the man closely. This was an unexpected turn of events—he couldn't let this opportunity slip by. If he could get close enough, he might glean valuable information about Viktor's plans.

Nikos greeted the man with a forced smile, trying to mask the tension that had suddenly filled the room. "What can I get you?"

Kurt leaned in, straining to hear their conversation as the man ordered a drink. "Just a beer. Been a long day," he said, his tone casual, but Kurt could sense an underlying urgency.

Kurt knew he needed to act quickly. He glanced around for a way to blend in without drawing attention to himself. As the man turned slightly, Kurt noticed a small group of tourists at a table nearby, laughing and enjoying their evening. This was his chance.

He slipped quietly over to the group, adopting a friendly demeanor. "Mind if I join you?" he asked, his voice cheerful.

The tourists welcomed him with warm smiles, eager to include someone new in their conversation. As they chatted, Kurt kept a watchful eye on the man at the bar, hoping to catch snippets of his conversation with Nikos.

"Are you from here?" one of the tourists asked, pulling Kurt back to the moment.

"Just passing through," Kurt replied, forcing a smile. "I've been exploring the island."

While maintaining his light-hearted conversation, he couldn't help but eavesdrop on the man. Nikos leaned in closer, speaking in hushed tones, clearly trying to keep the discussion discreet. Kurt's heart raced as he caught a few words: "Tonight," "meet," and "final preparations."

His pulse quickened; they were making plans, and Kurt had to find out where and when. Just then, the man finished his drink and turned back to Nikos, handing him some cash. "I'll be back in a bit," he said, shooting a glance around the room.

Kurt's opportunity was slipping away. "Excuse me," he said abruptly to the tourists, making a quick decision. "I need to step outside for a moment."

Without waiting for a response, he slipped out the door, just in time to see the man heading down a narrow alley behind the tavern. Kurt's instincts kicked in, and he followed, moving swiftly but quietly, hoping to remain undetected.

The alley was dimly lit, shadows dancing on the walls as he crept closer. The man had paused, glancing over his shoulder as if sensing he was being followed. Kurt pressed himself against the wall, heart racing as he prepared for a confrontation.

"Who's there?" the man called out, his voice low but commanding.

Kurt remained silent, every muscle coiled, ready to spring into action. He waited for the man to turn away, hoping for just a moment of distraction.

"Show yourself!" the man demanded, irritation creeping into his tone.

Kurt took a deep breath and stepped out of the shadows, his presence undeniable. "I'm the one asking the questions here," he said, his voice steady and confident.

The man's eyes widened in recognition, and he took a step back, sizing Kurt up. "You shouldn't be here," he warned, his bravado wavering slightly.

Kurt didn't hesitate. "What are you planning with Viktor? I know you're up to something."

The man narrowed his eyes, a flicker of fear dancing in their depths. "You don't know what you're getting into."

Kurt stepped forward, closing the distance. "Try me. You've already made a mistake by involving me."

The man hesitated, weighing his options. "You think you can intimidate me? You have no idea who you're dealing with."

Kurt leaned in closer, his voice low and dangerous. "I know exactly who I'm dealing with, and I won't let you or Viktor destroy this island."

The man's expression shifted, uncertainty creeping in. "Viktor doesn't take kindly to threats. You'll regret this."

Kurt's heart raced, but he remained calm. "I'm not afraid of him or you. Just tell me what you're planning, and maybe I can help you save yourself."

For a brief moment, the man seemed to consider it. Then, with a defiant shake of his head, he turned to flee deeper into the alley.

Kurt lunged forward, grabbing the man by the arm and spinning him around. "Don't make this harder than it needs to be."

"Let go of me!" the man shouted, struggling against Kurt's grip.

"Tell me where and when you're meeting Viktor," Kurt demanded, his voice firm. "This isn't a game. Lives are at stake."

The man's bravado faltered as he realized the seriousness of the situation. "Fine," he spat, still trying to wriggle free. "We're meeting at the old ruins at midnight. But you won't be able to stop us."

With that, he pulled away, breaking free from Kurt's grasp. Kurt watched as he darted down the alley, the man disappearing into the shadows.

Kurt stood there, the weight of the revelation settling in. Midnight at the ruins—it was a prime opportunity for Viktor and his associates to finalize their plans. He had to act fast.

He hurried back toward the tavern, his mind racing. With the information he had gathered, he needed to warn Nikos

Chapter 7

A battle of wits

The tavern was bustling with activity when Kurt returned, the atmosphere a stark contrast to the urgency that gripped him. Locals and tourists mingled, laughter filling the air, but Kurt felt a sense of isolation amidst the merriment. He had only minutes to warn Nikos about Viktor's plans, and every second counted.

He spotted Nikos behind the bar, serving drinks to a group of animated patrons. Kurt pushed through the throng, catching the old man's eye. "Nikos!" he called, urgency threading through his voice.

Nikos looked up, concern etched across his features as he wiped his hands on a towel. "Kurt, what's wrong?"

"They're meeting at the old ruins tonight at midnight. Viktor and his men. We need to come up with a plan to stop them," Kurt said, keeping his voice low to avoid drawing attention from the nearby patrons.

Nikos's expression darkened, the weight of the situation evident. "Midnight? That's dangerous. We should inform the police."

Kurt shook his head. "We can't involve the authorities. They won't understand the gravity of the situation. We have to handle this ourselves."

Nikos nodded slowly, the gravity of Kurt's words sinking in. "All right, but how do we stop them? They are armed and dangerous."

Kurt glanced around the tavern, his mind racing. "We'll need to be strategic. If we can gather information on their numbers and positions, we can set up an ambush."

"An ambush?" Nikos echoed, a hint of apprehension creeping into his voice. "That's risky."

"It's our best chance," Kurt insisted. "If we can catch them off guard, we can disrupt their plans and protect the island. We can't let them succeed."

Nikos studied Kurt for a moment, weighing the risk. "Okay. I'll rally some of the locals who know the area well. They can help us."

Kurt felt a flicker of hope. "Thank you, Nikos. We need to move quickly."

As they spoke, Kurt's mind raced with strategies. He thought of the terrain surrounding the old ruins—how to use it to their advantage. He'd need to get a headcount, assess the men's armaments, and devise a way to neutralize Viktor's influence without causing chaos.

"Gather the locals, and we'll meet back here in thirty minutes," Kurt instructed. "I'll scout the area and see what I can find out."

Nikos nodded, determination replacing the concern in his eyes. "Be careful, Kurt. You're going into the lion's den."

Kurt offered a reassuring smile, but inside, his heart thudded with the weight of the challenge ahead. He had to remain focused, keeping his emotions in check. Failure was not an option; too much was at stake.

With a final nod, Kurt slipped out of the tavern, the night air wrapping around him like a shroud. The streets were quieter now, the sounds of celebration fading into the distance as he made his way toward the ruins.

As he walked, he mentally prepared himself for what lay ahead. The old ruins were set on a hill overlooking the coast, a place steeped in history and mystery. They provided a perfect vantage point, but also served as a reminder of the ghosts he carried with him—echoes of the past that were woven into the fabric of his life.

When he arrived at the ruins, the moonlight illuminated the crumbling stone walls, casting long shadows that danced in the gentle breeze. Kurt crouched behind a cluster of rocks, surveying the area for any signs of activity. He needed to assess the situation without revealing his presence.

Minutes passed, and the tension in the air grew thick as he listened for any signs of Viktor and his men. He could feel the weight of his past bearing down on him, the memories threatening to resurface, but he pushed them aside. This was about the present—about protecting those who had welcomed him into their community.

Finally, he spotted movement in the distance. A group of figures approached the ruins, their silhouettes stark against the night sky. Kurt's heart raced as he leaned in closer, straining to hear their conversation.

"Tonight's the night," Viktor's voice echoed through the night, filled with a twisted sense of triumph. "We finalize our plans and take what's rightfully ours."

Kurt felt a surge of anger but remained hidden, focusing on gathering information. The group was larger than he expected—at least six men, all armed and ready for a fight.

"We need to be quick," one of Viktor's associates said. "We can't risk being seen."

Kurt's mind raced. They were clearly plotting something significant, and he needed to disrupt their plans before it was too late. He glanced around, searching for potential advantages in the terrain.

As he assessed the area, he spotted a small cave to the right of the ruins. If he could reach it, he could position himself closer without being seen. With stealth and purpose, he made his way toward the cave, careful to stay low and out of sight.

Once inside, Kurt settled in, the darkness enveloping him like a protective blanket. From this vantage point, he could hear everything—the low murmurs of Viktor and his associates as they laid out their plans. He focused on memorizing their movements, their discussions growing more intense.

"Once we secure the shipment, we'll be unstoppable," Viktor said, his voice dripping with arrogance. "The island will be ours for the taking."

Kurt clenched his fists, anger boiling beneath the surface. He had to act, but he couldn't rush in blindly. He needed to gather more intelligence, understand their operations before making a move.

The minutes dragged on, each second stretching into an eternity as Kurt listened, formulating a plan in his mind. He could hear the men discussing logistics, security details, and possible escape routes. Every detail was a thread he could use to weave his strategy.

Suddenly, he heard footsteps approaching the cave entrance. Kurt's breath caught in his throat as he braced himself, ready to defend against an unexpected confrontation.

The footsteps stopped just outside, and a shadow fell across the entrance. Kurt held his breath, waiting to see if he'd been discovered. He felt the tension in the air, the anticipation hanging heavy as he prepared for the worst.

The figure lingered for a moment, then turned and walked away, oblivious to his presence. Kurt exhaled slowly, relief washing over him as he returned his focus to the group outside.

As he peered through the cave entrance, he knew he had to act soon. With Viktor's plans now clear, it was time to put his own into motion. He would gather the locals and prepare for an ambush, using the element of surprise to his advantage.

Tonight would be a battle of wits—a chance to outmaneuver his old enemy and protect the island he had come to love. With renewed determination, Kurt prepared to return to Nikos, ready to turn the tide in their favor.

Chapter 8:

The Showdown

The clock in the old church tower struck midnight as Kurt emerged from the cave, adrenaline coursing through his veins. The night was thick with tension, and the air crackled with anticipation. He had gathered a small group of locals—fellow villagers who cared about the island's safety—and they were ready to confront Viktor and his men.

Kurt made his way back down the hill toward the ruins, his heart pounding in rhythm with his footsteps. He knew that this was not just about him; it was about standing up for the community that had welcomed him into their midst. The stakes were high, and he couldn't afford to let fear dictate his actions.

As he approached the ruins, he spotted the flickering glow of lanterns illuminating the area. The faint murmurs of Viktor's men echoed in the night, their voices tinged with urgency. Kurt slipped into the shadows, positioning himself behind a cluster of ancient stones that had once formed the foundation of the old temple.

From his vantage point, he could see Viktor and his associates gathered around a makeshift table. Maps and plans were spread out before them, the dim light casting eerie shadows across their faces. Kurt strained to hear their conversation.

"We need to finalize the shipment details tonight," Viktor was saying, his voice laced with impatience. "If we delay, we risk being discovered. We can't let that happen."

Kurt felt a surge of anger at the thought of Viktor's ambitions threatening the island. This was more than just a personal vendetta; it was a chance to protect everything he had come to love.

He glanced behind him to see the locals had assembled, their faces set with determination. Nikos stood at the forefront, a makeshift weapon in hand—a sturdy length of wood that spoke to his resolve. Kurt gave a subtle nod to signal them to stay quiet and prepare for action.

As Viktor continued to speak, Kurt focused on the maps spread before him. He needed to gather intelligence on their plans, but the opportunity was fleeting. The moment Viktor dismissed his men or turned his back would be the moment to act.

Suddenly, one of the men leaned closer to Viktor, whispering urgently. "What about the locals? We can't have them snooping around."

Viktor waved a dismissive hand. "They're just a bunch of farmers and fishermen. They won't dare interfere. But just to be safe, let's send someone to keep watch. I want to know if they even think about causing trouble."

Kurt's heart raced. This was the moment he had been waiting for. He had to disrupt their plans before they could tighten their grip on the island.

"Now!" Kurt whispered to the locals, motioning for them to follow him. They moved silently, fanning out to surround the area, each person taking position behind rocks and trees, ready to act at a moment's notice.

As Kurt crept closer, he heard Viktor continue to bark orders, oblivious to the danger creeping toward him. Kurt steadied his breath, focusing on the task at hand. He had trained for moments like this, where strategy and strength converged in a single instant.

"Let's go!" Kurt shouted, his voice breaking the tense silence as he lunged from his hiding place. The locals surged forward behind him, catching Viktor and his men off guard.

The confusion that followed was electric. Kurt pushed through the chaos, locking eyes with Viktor, whose expression shifted from surprise to fury.

"What is the meaning of this?" Viktor roared, his face contorting with rage.

"We're taking back our island," Kurt declared, his voice steady as he faced his old nemesis.

Viktor's men scrambled, trying to regain their composure, but the advantage was with Kurt and his allies. The locals, fueled by a mix of fear and determination, rushed forward, brandishing makeshift weapons.

Kurt's instincts kicked in as he moved through the fray, dodging blows and countering with swift strikes. He could feel the adrenaline pulsing through him, a familiar rush that reminded him of the battles fought long ago. But this time, he was fighting for something greater than himself.

Viktor lunged at Kurt, rage fueling his every move. "You think you can stop me? I will not be denied!"

Kurt met Viktor's attack head-on, their fists colliding with a force that echoed through the night. The world around them faded as they fell into a rhythm of combat, each movement a dance of power and resilience.

With every blow exchanged, Kurt remembered the faces of his comrades, the sacrifices made, and the lives lost. He refused to let Viktor's ambitions ruin everything he had worked to build.

As they fought, Kurt could feel the tide of battle shifting. The locals were gaining ground, pushing Viktor's men back with sheer determination. It was a testament to the strength of a community united against a common threat.

Kurt landed a powerful punch to Viktor's midsection, sending him staggering back. "This ends tonight!" he shouted, his voice filled with conviction.

Viktor's eyes widened, realization dawning. "You think you can defeat me? I have resources, allies—"

"I have something you'll never understand," Kurt interrupted, stepping forward, fueled by a surge of determination. "I fight for something bigger than myself. I fight for this island, for these people."

Viktor snarled, wiping blood from his lip. "You're a fool, Kurt. You think you can just walk away from your past? You're still that soldier hiding behind a facade."

Kurt's jaw clenched. "And you're still the same coward trying to control everything through fear. It's over, Viktor."

With that, he lunged forward, his movements fluid and precise. Kurt's training had never left him, and as he delivered a series of rapid blows, he could feel the weight of his past lifting. Each strike was a step toward closure, a way to reclaim his life from the shadows.

Viktor struggled to keep up, desperation fueling his attacks. But Kurt was relentless, pushing him back toward the edge of the ruins, the moonlight casting a stark glow on their fight.

Finally, with a swift maneuver, Kurt disarmed Viktor, sending his weapon clattering to the ground. Viktor stumbled, losing his balance as he fell back against the ancient stones.

Kurt stood over him, breathing heavily, the tension in the air palpable. "It's time to let go, Viktor. You can't control everything."

As Viktor looked up, the fight had gone out of him. The realization of defeat washed over his features, a mixture of anger and resignation. "You think this is over? I'll find a way to come back," he spat, the venom in his voice a last desperate attempt to assert dominance.

Kurt shook his head, a calm determination settling over him. "Not this time. You've lost, and you need to leave Kos. If you don't, you'll face the consequences."

As the locals closed in, ready to support Kurt, Viktor's demeanor shifted. He understood the gravity of his situation, the realization that his influence on the island had been shattered.

"Fine," he said, his voice now devoid of the bravado it once held. "But this isn't over. You'll regret this day, Kurt."

Kurt watched as Viktor backed away, retreating into the shadows of the night, leaving behind the remnants of his failed ambitions. The tension began to dissipate as the locals cheered, relief washing over the group. They had faced down a formidable enemy and emerged victorious.

As Kurt stood amidst his newfound allies, he felt a sense of camaraderie and purpose that he hadn't experienced in years. They had come together to protect their home, and in doing so, Kurt had rediscovered a piece of himself he thought he had lost forever.

But as the adrenaline faded, a shadow of concern lingered in his heart. Viktor was still out there, and while he had been defeated tonight, Kurt knew he would not give up easily. The battle might be won, but the war for peace on Kos was far from over.

Chapter 9:

The Revelation

As the dust began to settle from the confrontation at the ruins, Kurt took a moment to absorb the victory they had achieved. The locals were buzzing with excitement, their spirits lifted by the camaraderie and shared purpose that had united them against Viktor and his men. They celebrated their newfound strength, but Kurt remained on high alert, aware that the battle was only half won.

Nikos approached him, a broad smile on his face. "You fought well, Kurt! We couldn't have done this without you."

Kurt nodded, grateful for the old man's support, but his thoughts were clouded by the looming uncertainty. "Thank you, Nikos. But we need to remain vigilant. Viktor won't just walk away quietly."

The tavern owner's smile faded, replaced by a furrowed brow. "You're right. He's not the type to give up easily. We should prepare for what comes next."

As the group began to disperse, Kurt gathered the remaining locals, eager to discuss their next steps. They moved to a more secluded area away from the ruins, where the flickering lantern light cast long shadows against the walls.

"We need to ensure that Viktor doesn't come back," Kurt said, scanning the faces of those around him. "He'll likely regroup and plan his revenge. We need to be ready."

One of the younger men, a fisherman named Dimitris, stepped forward. "But how do we prepare? He has resources, and we are just villagers."

Kurt held his gaze, willing to instill confidence. "We may not have weapons or a militia, but we have each other and knowledge of this island. We know the terrain, the routes—how to use our home to our advantage."

Nikos nodded in agreement. "We can create a network of lookouts, keep an eye on the harbor and the old hotel. If he tries to come back, we'll know."

As they discussed their plan, a sense of purpose emerged within the group. The fear that had once clouded their lives began to dissipate, replaced by the resolve to protect their home. Kurt felt a swell of pride for the community that had rallied around him, for the strength they shared in the face of adversity.

Just as they were about to finalize their plans, a voice cut through the chatter. "You think you've won, don't you?"

Kurt turned, heart dropping at the familiar voice. Viktor had returned, his presence shrouded in darkness, eyes glinting with malice. "You've put on quite the show tonight, but you don't understand the game we're playing."

Kurt stepped forward, positioning himself between Viktor and the group. "What do you want, Viktor? You're not welcome here."

The corner of Viktor's mouth curled into a sardonic smile. "Oh, but I think I am. You see, I'm not here for a fight. I'm here for a negotiation."

Kurt's stomach churned. "What kind of negotiation could we possibly have? You're the one who threatened our home."

Viktor shrugged, feigning indifference. "That's business. But let's not focus on the past. You've shown me tonight that you're a formidable opponent, and I respect that. I'm willing to offer you a deal."

The locals tensed, exchanging wary glances. Kurt felt the weight of their apprehension, but he couldn't show fear. "What kind of deal?"

Viktor stepped closer, his voice lowering to a conspiratorial whisper. "You have something I want—knowledge of this island, connections, resources. If you help me find a way to secure my shipments, I'll leave you and your precious village alone. No more threats, no more violence."

Kurt clenched his fists, his mind racing. "You think I'd ever ally with you? You're a criminal. We'll never help you."

Viktor's expression hardened. "Think carefully, Kurt. I have my ways of making life difficult. I'm not just a ghost from your past— I have connections everywhere. You may think you're safe here, but I can change that in an instant."

Kurt met Viktor's gaze, feeling the weight of the threat hanging in the air. "If you think I'll betray my home for your empty promises, you're mistaken. We will not be intimidated."

Viktor chuckled darkly, the sound sending a chill down Kurt's spine. "You misunderstand me. This isn't a threat—it's a warning. You're playing a dangerous game, and the stakes are higher than you realize."

With that, Viktor turned on his heel and walked away, disappearing into the night like a shadow. The tension in the air hung heavy as the locals exchanged nervous glances, unsure of what the encounter meant for their future.

Kurt stood there, the adrenaline from the earlier confrontation mixing with the frustration of Viktor's words. "We need to prepare. He'll come back, and we must be ready for whatever he has planned," he declared, his voice steady despite the turmoil churning within.

As they discussed their next steps, Kurt's mind raced. He knew they couldn't trust Viktor; his offer was a façade, a trap designed to exploit their fears. But he also felt a sense of urgency. Viktor's threat was real, and the safety of the island depended on their ability to outmaneuver him.

Hours passed as they strategized, the group mapping out potential lookout points and emergency routes. Kurt found himself immersed in the planning, the camaraderie of the villagers lifting his spirits. They shared stories, laughter, and a resolve that fortified their bond.

But beneath the surface, the seeds of doubt began to take root in Kurt's mind. What if Viktor returned with more resources? What if they weren't prepared for the full extent of his wrath? The thoughts gnawed at him, a constant reminder of the fragility of their situation.

As the night wore on, Kurt excused himself, needing a moment of solitude to collect his thoughts. He wandered down to the edge of the harbor, the moonlight shimmering on the water. The gentle lapping of the waves calmed his racing heart, but the sense of unease remained.

He stared out at the horizon, reflecting on the choices that had led him to this moment. The memories of his past—the lives he had taken, the battles fought—played in his mind like a haunting melody. He had escaped the chaos of his old life, but it seemed it had followed him here, ready to erupt once more.

Suddenly, a figure appeared beside him. It was Nikos, his expression somber. "Kurt, are you all right?"

Kurt turned, forcing a smile despite the heaviness in his chest. "I'm fine, just thinking."

Nikos nodded, his gaze shifting to the water. "Viktor is dangerous. You know that, right? He won't stop until he gets what he wants."

"I know," Kurt replied, frustration simmering just below the surface. "I just can't shake the feeling that he has something bigger planned. It's not just about the shipments."

Nikos studied him for a moment. "You're right. He's a man who doesn't play games lightly. We need to stay one step ahead of him."

Kurt took a deep breath, the salty air filling his lungs. "We will. But I need to know what he's planning. We have to uncover the truth."

As they stood there in silence, a thought struck Kurt. "What if we could infiltrate his operation? Find out more about his connections and his plans?"

Nikos raised an eyebrow, a glimmer of hope in his eyes. "You mean—"

"Exactly," Kurt interrupted, excitement sparking within him. "If we could get someone close to him, we could gather vital information and turn the tables."

Nikos considered the idea, his expression thoughtful. "It's a risky move, but it could work. But who do we send? We need someone who can blend in, someone he wouldn't suspect."

Kurt pondered for a moment, his mind racing through possibilities. "What about the tourists? They've been here for a while, and some may have connections. If we could convince them to help…"

Nikos nodded slowly, his eyes brightening with the prospect. "It's worth a shot. But we'll need to approach it delicately. We can't let Viktor catch wind of our intentions."

With renewed purpose, Kurt and Nikos returned to the group, eager to share their plan. As they discussed the logistics of infiltrating Viktor's operation, Kurt felt a shift within himself—a sense of clarity and determination.

Tonight had revealed the depth of the threat they faced, but it had also sparked a fire within him. He would not let Viktor destroy the life he had built on Kos. They would outsmart him, turning the very tactics he used against others back on him.

As they laid the groundwork for their plan, Kurt knew that the real battle was just beginning. It would require cunning, bravery, and a willingness to confront the ghosts of the past. But he was ready; he would fight for his home, for his new family, and for the chance to reclaim his life from the shadows.

Chapter 10:

Acceptance and Closure

As dawn broke over Kos, a new day dawned, bringing with it a sense of urgency. Kurt stood at the edge of his terrace, the soft light painting the landscape in hues of gold and pink. The island that had once felt like a sanctuary now bore the weight of impending conflict. He inhaled deeply, trying to steady the swirling emotions within him.

After a restless night spent planning with Nikos and the locals, Kurt knew they needed to act quickly. Infiltrating Viktor's operation would not only provide them with crucial information but also help restore a sense of normalcy to their lives. The stakes were higher than ever, and the fear of what lay ahead hung heavily in the air.

As Kurt prepared to meet with the group, his mind drifted back to the confrontation with Viktor. He had faced his past head-on, and while it had been a victory of sorts, the shadows of regret still lingered. The memories of lost comrades, of choices that had led to pain and suffering, gnawed at him.

Stepping back inside, he gathered his gear—an old backpack filled with essentials he had kept since his days in the SAS. As he prepared to leave, he caught a glimpse of himself in the mirror. The man staring back was a far cry from the soldier he once was; he was now a protector, a guardian of this island and its people.

When Kurt arrived at the designated meeting point, a small clearing in the forest just outside the village, he found the locals gathered, their expressions a mix of determination and trepidation. Nikos stood at the forefront, ready to address the group.

"Thank you all for coming," he began, his voice steady. "We stand at a crossroads. The threat we face is real, but together we have the strength to confront it."

Kurt stepped forward, feeling the weight of their gaze upon him. "We've come up with a plan to gather information on Viktor and his associates. It's time we take the fight to them."

The group listened intently as Kurt outlined their strategy. They would use the tourists as a means of infiltration, engaging with Viktor's crew in a way that would seem innocuous but would allow them to gather vital intelligence.

"We need to be smart about this," Kurt cautioned. "Viktor is cunning. He won't hesitate to eliminate anyone who poses a threat to his plans. We must act with caution."

As they discussed the details, Kurt felt a flicker of hope. For the first time since

Viktor's arrival, he sensed that they could reclaim their lives and protect their home. But beneath that hope lay an undercurrent of fear—what if their plan failed? What if someone got hurt?

Nikos approached Kurt, placing a reassuring hand on his shoulder. "We're with you, Kurt. Whatever happens, we face it together."

Kurt nodded, appreciating the solidarity of his friends and neighbors. "Thank you, Nikos. I'll do everything in my power to ensure your safety."

As they finalized their plan, a sense of purpose began to wash over Kurt, dispelling the shadows of his past. He wasn't just fighting for himself; he was fighting for the community that had embraced him, for the chance to create a future unmarred by the ghosts of yesterday.

Later that afternoon, Kurt and a small group of locals made their way to the taverna, where a group of tourists was gathered, laughing and enjoying the warm sun. Among them were several he had seen with Viktor the night before.

As they entered the bustling tavern, Kurt felt a rush of apprehension, but he steeled himself, recalling the camaraderie they had built. They would need to act naturally, to blend in and establish trust with the tourists.

"Just be yourselves," he whispered to his companions. "We need them to feel comfortable."

Kurt approached a table where a group of tourists sat, their laughter infectious. "Mind if I join you?" he asked with a smile.

The tourists welcomed him, eager to share stories of their travels. Kurt engaged them in conversation, carefully gauging their responses and subtly steering the dialogue toward their experiences on the island.

As they talked, Kurt caught glimpses of Viktor's associates lingering at the bar, watching him closely. The tension coiled within him, but he maintained his composure, refusing to show any sign of anxiety.

"You guys have been here for a while, right?" Kurt asked, feigning casual interest. "What do you think of the island? Any adventures planned?"

One of the tourists, a woman with bright eyes named Eleni, smiled widely. "It's beautiful! We're planning to visit the old ruins later today. I've heard they're quite magical."

Kurt felt a flicker of alarm at the mention of the ruins. "Ah, yes. The ruins have a lot of history. Just be cautious—there are some old stories about the place."

"Old stories?" another tourist chimed in, leaning forward. "Like what?"

Kurt hesitated, choosing his words carefully. "Well, some say it's a place where deals are made—some good, some not so good. Just be aware of who you trust out there."

The tourists exchanged glances, their excitement tempered by Kurt's caution. He sensed they were beginning to take his words seriously, which was precisely what he needed.

As the conversation continued, Kurt skillfully gathered more information, subtly probing for connections and backgrounds. He learned that some of the tourists had connections to local businesses, potentially opening doors for him to learn more about Viktor's operations.

But just as he began to feel confident in their approach, Viktor's associates moved closer, their eyes narrowing as they watched the interactions unfold. Kurt's heart raced—this was the moment they had to capitalize on.

As the sun began to set, casting long shadows across the tavern, Kurt knew they had to act soon. "Eleni, would you like to join me for a walk by the harbor? I could show you some hidden spots," he offered, gauging her interest.

Her eyes sparkled with excitement. "I'd love that!"

As they made their way outside, Kurt felt the weight of the moment. He had to draw Viktor's associates away from the group, to create an opportunity for the locals to gather the intelligence they needed.

Once at the harbor, Kurt glanced back at the taverna, ensuring his allies were in place. He turned to Eleni, keeping his tone light. "So, tell me—what brings you to Kos? What are you hoping to find?"

As they walked along the water's edge, the soft waves lapping at the shore, Kurt felt a sense of calm settling over him. In that moment, he realized that he was no longer just a soldier haunted by his past. He was part of something bigger—a community united against a common threat.

But just as he began to relax, a familiar figure emerged from the shadows behind him. Viktor stepped into view, his expression dark and menacing, eyes locked onto Kurt with an intensity that sent a chill down his spine.

"Kurt," Viktor said, his voice dripping with mockery. "I see you've found some new friends."

Kurt's heart raced as he turned to face Viktor, aware that the precarious balance he had worked so hard to maintain was crumbling. "What do you want, Viktor?"

The older man's smile widened, a twisted satisfaction gleaming in his eyes. "You should have accepted my offer. Now you've put yourself—and everyone around you—in danger."

Kurt felt the tension thicken in the air, but he stood his ground. "You won't intimidate me. I will protect this island, no matter what."

Viktor's gaze flickered to Eleni, and Kurt's stomach dropped. "Oh, I have no intention of hurting anyone...yet. But I think it's time you learn what true danger really is."

With that, Viktor gestured, and his associates emerged from the shadows, surrounding Kurt and Eleni. The realization hit Kurt like a punch to the gut; they were outnumbered, and the confrontation was about to escalate.

"Get away from her!" Kurt shouted, stepping protectively in front of Eleni.

Viktor's men grinned, closing in on them. "You really thought you could protect everyone, Kurt?" Viktor taunted. "You've set yourself up for failure."

As tension hung heavy in the air, Kurt realized he had to act fast. This was not just a fight for survival; it was a fight for everything he had come to care about.

"Run!" he shouted to Eleni, adrenaline surging through him as he prepared to face Viktor and his men.

But as she hesitated, a look of determination in her eyes, Kurt knew they were in this together. They would face the threat head-on, drawing on the strength of the community they had forged.

"Together," she said, stepping beside him.

In that moment of unity, Kurt felt a renewed sense of purpose. He would not let Viktor tear apart the life he had built. They would fight together, and no matter what happened next, they would face it as a united front.

Chapter 11:

The Revelation

The air was thick with tension as Kurt faced Viktor and his associates, adrenaline coursing through his veins. He had fought for peace and had brought Eleni into a situation that was quickly spiraling out of control.

Viktor's men tightened their circle, their intentions clear. Kurt's heart raced, but he felt a sense of resolve. He wasn't just fighting for himself; he was fighting for Eleni, for the community of Kos, and for the chance to reclaim his life from the shadows.

"Enough games, Kurt," Viktor sneered, stepping forward. "You've meddled in affairs far beyond your understanding. This is your last chance to walk away."

"Walk away?" Kurt echoed, a fierce defiance igniting within him. "You think I'd let you threaten this island and its people without a fight? I won't back down."

Eleni stood resolutely beside him, her eyes filled with determination. "You don't scare us, Viktor. We will stand our ground."

Viktor's smile faltered for just a moment, but it was enough for Kurt to see the flicker of uncertainty behind his bravado. "You're making a grave mistake. You think you're ready for this?"

"More ready than you realize," Kurt replied, a fire igniting in his chest. "We know what you're planning. You won't succeed here."

With a wave of his hand, Viktor signaled his men to move closer, a smirk returning to his lips. "I have resources, connections. You're just a few villagers playing hero."

Kurt's pulse quickened, but he refused to show any sign of fear. "You underestimate us.

We know this island, and we know how to fight for it."

With a sudden move, Viktor lunged forward, and Kurt reacted instinctively, stepping aside just in time. A scuffle erupted as Viktor's men charged, and Kurt felt Eleni's presence beside him, steady and strong.

"Stay close!" Kurt shouted, throwing a punch at one of the attackers while sidestepping another. The fight erupted into chaos as the shadows of the night came alive with shouts and the sound of bodies colliding.

Kurt fought with precision and agility, drawing on every lesson learned during his years of service. He could feel the weight of the past fueling his every movement, transforming pain into purpose. He dodged a punch and countered with a swift kick, sending one of Viktor's men sprawling to the ground.

As the fight unfolded, Kurt glanced at Eleni, who was holding her own against another assailant. They had become a team, united against a common threat. The adrenaline surging through him only fueled his determination.

But as the chaos swirled around them, Viktor managed to pull himself back into the fray, his eyes dark with rage. "You think you can defy me?" he bellowed, the anger twisting his features. "You have no idea what I'm capable of!"

With renewed fury, he lunged at Kurt, and the two men collided, grappling fiercely. The world around them blurred as they fought, each man trying to assert dominance over the other.

Kurt could feel the sweat pouring down his back, the strain of the fight weighing heavily on him. But he refused to give in; this was a battle not just of strength but of wills. As Viktor pressed forward, Kurt fought back, channeling the energy of the moment, remembering every loss and every sacrifice that had led him here.

"You were always a coward, Viktor!" Kurt shouted, pushing against his adversary with all his might. "Hiding behind others, using fear to control. That ends now!"

With a sudden burst of strength, Kurt broke free from Viktor's grip, sending him staggering backward. The momentary advantage gave Kurt a chance to gather his thoughts. He could see Eleni fighting fiercely, but they were still outnumbered.

"Regroup!" Kurt called out, his voice rising above the chaos. "We need to create space!"

As his allies began to pull back, forming a defensive line, Kurt took a deep breath, focusing on the task ahead. Viktor's men were relentless, but they lacked the unity that Kurt and the villagers had forged.

Kurt turned his attention to Eleni, who was now beside him, breathless but unyielding.

"Are you okay?" he asked, concern etched on his face.

"I'm fine. We need to finish this," she replied, her determination unwavering.

Kurt nodded, realizing that they had to outsmart their opponents. "We can't let them corner us. We need to use the terrain to our advantage."

With a swift motion, Kurt pointed to the rocky outcrop nearby. "We can create an obstacle. If we can force them into the open, we can take them one by one."

Eleni's eyes lit up with understanding. "I'll help you. We can draw them in."

As they prepared their strategy, Viktor's men began to close in again, sensing that their advantage was slipping. Kurt's heart raced as he and Eleni readied themselves for the next wave of attackers.

"Now!" Kurt shouted, signaling to the others to create a diversion. As the locals began to push forward, Kurt and Eleni darted to the side, leading Viktor's men toward the rocky outcrop.

The plan unfolded quickly, the chaos of the battle swirling around them. Kurt moved with purpose, dodging and weaving as he forced the attackers to follow him into the narrow space between the rocks.

"Keep moving!" he urged, adrenaline fueling his every step. Eleni stayed close, matching his pace as they maneuvered their way through the terrain.

Suddenly, Viktor's men found themselves trapped, caught between the rocks and the furious onslaught of Kurt and the villagers. The tide had turned, and the momentum shifted in their favor.

As the fight reached its climax, Kurt felt the weight of the battle pressing down on him, but he refused to falter. With every strike, every punch, he fought not just for himself but for the island and the community he had come to love.

Finally, after what felt like an eternity, Viktor's men began to retreat, their confidence shattered. Kurt stood tall amidst the chaos, adrenaline surging through him as he caught Viktor's gaze, the man's bravado fading into fear.

"This isn't over!" Viktor shouted, backing away as his remaining men fled into the shadows.

Kurt stood his ground, breathing heavily as he faced Viktor. "You're right. It's just the beginning. But you will not win here."

Viktor glared at him, a mixture of anger and defeat in his eyes. "You may have won this battle, but I'll find a way to return."

With that, Viktor turned and disappeared into the night, leaving behind the remnants of his ambitions and the fading echoes of the confrontation.

Kurt let out a deep breath, the adrenaline slowly fading as reality settled in. They had done it; they had stood together and faced the threat head-on. The villagers rallied around him, cheers of triumph filling the air.

As Kurt looked at Eleni, gratitude swelled within him. "Thank you for standing by me," he said, his voice sincere. "We couldn't have done this without you."

She smiled, her eyes bright with determination. "We fought together. This island is our home, and we'll protect it."

As the villagers celebrated their victory, Kurt felt a sense of closure beginning to wash over him. The past had haunted him for far too long, but now he had taken a stand—not just for himself, but for those who had come to trust him.

He knew that Viktor might return, that the shadows of the past would always linger, but Kurt was ready to face whatever came next. He had found a new purpose, a new community, and for the first time in years, he felt truly at peace.

Chapter 12:

Embracing Peace

The sun rose over Kos, casting a warm glow across the village. The air was crisp and fresh, a stark contrast to the chaos of the night before. As Kurt stood on his terrace, the events of the previous evening played through his mind like a vivid dream. They had faced down Viktor and his men, reclaiming their island and forging a stronger bond with the community.

Kurt took a deep breath, letting the tranquility of the morning settle into his bones. The battle had not only been a confrontation with external forces; it had also marked a significant turning point within himself. He felt lighter, as if a weight he had carried for years had finally begun to lift.

After the confrontation, the locals had gathered at the taverna, sharing stories and laughter, celebrating their victory. Kurt had watched them with a sense of pride and belonging, realizing how far he had come since arriving on the island as a solitary figure. They were no longer just villagers; they were friends and allies who had come together for a common cause.

As the day unfolded, Kurt decided to visit the church he had tended to during his time on Kos. The old stone structure stood tall against the backdrop of the mountains, a symbol of hope and resilience. He climbed the familiar path, each step a reminder of the journey he had taken.

When he arrived, the church was peaceful, the morning light filtering through the stained glass windows and casting colorful patterns on the floor. Kurt stepped inside, taking a moment to soak in the serenity of the space. He moved to the altar, lighting a candle and offering a silent prayer of gratitude for the community he had found.

As he stood there, he felt a sense of closure wash over him. The ghosts of his past—his regrets, his losses—no longer held the same power over him. He had confronted his demons and emerged stronger, ready to embrace the future.

Just then, the sound of footsteps echoed behind him. Kurt turned to see Eleni entering the church, her expression brightening at the sight of him. "I figured I'd find you here," she said with a smile. "I came to thank you for everything."

Kurt chuckled softly, the warmth of her presence filling the space. "You don't need to thank me. You were brave out there. We did this together."

Eleni moved closer, her eyes sparkling with determination. "But you were the one who led us. You showed us how to stand up for ourselves, to fight for what we believe in."

"I couldn't have done it without your support," Kurt replied, feeling the weight of her words. "You gave me strength when I needed it the most."

They stood in comfortable silence for a moment, the weight of their shared experiences hanging between them. Kurt felt a warmth spreading in his chest, a connection that went beyond words.

"What's next for you, Kurt?" Eleni asked, breaking the silence. "Now that the threat has been dealt with, what do you plan to do?"

Kurt paused, contemplating the question. "I want to help the island heal. There's a lot of work to be done, and I want to be part of that. I've found a purpose here that I didn't think was possible."

Eleni nodded, her expression thoughtful. "You belong here, Kurt. You've become part of this community, and we need someone like you."

As they walked together outside, the sun illuminated the path ahead, and Kurt felt a renewed sense of hope. They strolled through the village, greeting neighbors and exchanging smiles, the bond of their shared struggle bringing them closer together.

Days turned into weeks as Kurt immersed himself in community life. He organized clean-up efforts to restore the village, taught self-defense workshops for those interested, and even helped with the local fishing fleet. With each task, he felt more rooted, more connected to the people and the land.

But the past lingered, too, like a shadow that refused to fade entirely. Kurt often found himself reflecting on the losses he had endured, the lives he had touched and those who had been lost along the way. He carried their memories with him, but now, instead of a burden, they served as a reminder of why he fought for peace.

One evening, as the sun dipped below the horizon, casting a warm glow across the sky, Kurt gathered the locals for a community dinner by the harbor. The air was filled with the enticing aroma of grilled fish and fresh bread, laughter echoing against the backdrop of the sea.

As they shared stories and food, Kurt felt a deep sense of belonging. He listened to the tales of resilience, of families coming together, and of the shared vision for a brighter future. It was a tapestry woven with hope and strength, and Kurt was proud to be a part of it.

As the night wore on, Kurt stood up to address the group, a smile spreading across his face. "I want to thank you all for welcoming me into your community. You've shown me what it means to fight for something greater than oneself, to embrace the bonds of friendship and solidarity."

The villagers cheered, their spirits high, and Kurt felt a warmth spread through him. He realized that this was his new family, a group of people willing to stand together against any threat.

"And while we've faced challenges together," he continued, "I believe our greatest strength lies in our unity. Let's continue to support one another, to work together, and to protect this beautiful island we call home."

As the night deepened and stars began to twinkle overhead, Kurt felt a profound sense of peace settle within him. The battles of his past no longer defined him; instead, he had forged a new path, one filled with purpose, hope, and a community that embraced him.

With laughter and joy echoing around him, Kurt finally felt at home.

Chapter 13:

The Power of Compounding

The sun rose gently over Kos, painting the landscape in hues of soft gold. Kurt stood on his terrace, sipping coffee as he gazed out at the tranquil sea. The chaos of the past weeks had faded, replaced by a sense of normalcy that felt almost surreal. The community had united to strengthen their defenses and build a brighter future, and Kurt had found his place within it.

As he savored the moment, Kurt's thoughts drifted to the lessons he had learned throughout his journey. Each challenge had contributed to his growth, and he realized that the most profound changes often came from the smallest actions. The power of compounding—an idea he had once encountered during his years of training—had taken on a new meaning in his life.

He remembered how small, consistent efforts could lead to significant results. Just as in finance, where compound interest builds wealth over time, the cumulative effect of their community's actions was creating a stronghold against adversity. Together, they were fortifying their bonds and resources, ensuring that Kos would thrive.

Kurt had worked tirelessly alongside the locals, not only to secure the island but also to rebuild trust and camaraderie. They had transformed fear into action, learning to rely on one another. He had witnessed firsthand how their collective efforts blossomed into something extraordinary.

With renewed purpose, Kurt decided to take the lessons of compounding further. He gathered the villagers for a community meeting in the taverna, eager to share his thoughts. The atmosphere buzzed with anticipation as familiar faces filled the room, laughter and chatter echoing against the walls.

"Thank you all for coming," Kurt began, standing at the front of the room. "I've been reflecting on our journey and the power of what we've achieved together. Every small action we take, every moment we invest in our community, compounds over time."

Nikos nodded, his expression encouraging. "That's right, Kurt. Every effort counts, no matter how small."

Kurt smiled, heartened by the support. "I believe we can harness this power to create a more sustainable future for Kos. We've proven we can come together in times of crisis, but let's focus on how we can thrive in peace."

The crowd leaned in, interest piqued. Kurt outlined a vision for the future—community gardens that would provide fresh produce, workshops to teach new skills, and initiatives to promote local businesses. "If we invest in ourselves and support one another, we'll build a resilient economy that can withstand any challenge."

As he spoke, enthusiasm ignited among the villagers. Ideas flowed freely, and suggestions for various projects poured in. From eco-tourism to cultural festivals, the group brainstormed ways to enhance their community and draw visitors to the island.

"This is just the beginning," Kurt said, feeling the energy in the room. "Imagine how much we can achieve if we keep working together, compounding our efforts into something truly remarkable."

Nikos raised his glass, a broad smile on his face. "To our future and the strength of our community!"

The room erupted in cheers, a wave of optimism washing over them. Kurt felt a profound sense of belonging as he joined the villagers in their celebration. This was the life he had fought for—a life filled with purpose, connection, and hope.

In the following weeks, Kurt and the locals launched various initiatives, each building upon the foundation they had created together. The community garden flourished, providing fresh vegetables that brought healthy meals to their tables. Workshops were organized to teach skills ranging from fishing techniques to crafting, fostering a spirit of collaboration and shared learning.

As they worked side by side, Kurt felt a sense of fulfillment. Each small victory—every vegetable harvested, every skill learned—added to the growing tapestry of their lives. The power of compounding had taken root in their hearts, creating a sense of pride and ownership over their future.

One afternoon, while tending to the garden, Kurt received a visit from Eleni. She approached with a smile, her hair catching the sunlight as she wiped her brow. "Kurt, you won't believe the interest we've received about the upcoming festival!"

Kurt turned, intrigued. "Really? What kind of interest?"

"People are excited! We've had inquiries from nearby islands, and even some from the mainland who want to participate," Eleni replied, her enthusiasm infectious.

Kurt felt a rush of excitement. "That's incredible! This festival will not only showcase our culture but also draw more visitors to Kos. It's a perfect opportunity to highlight everything we've built together."

"Yes, and it's a chance to show that we're not just a quiet village—we're a community ready to thrive," Eleni added, her eyes sparkling with passion.

As the festival approached, the island buzzed with activity. Villagers worked together to prepare, each person contributing their unique talents. Kurt felt a sense of pride swell within him as he watched the transformation take place.

On the day of the festival, the village was alive with color and laughter. Stalls lined the streets, showcasing handmade crafts, delicious foods, and cultural displays. The air was filled with the sounds of music and the scents of grilled fish and roasted vegetables.

As Kurt moved through the crowd, he marveled at the unity of the villagers. They were no longer just individuals; they had become a collective force, each person's contribution enriching the experience for everyone.

Eleni joined him, her smile radiant as she took in the festivities. "This is amazing, Kurt! Look at everyone coming together."

Kurt nodded, his heart swelling with gratitude. "It's a testament to what we've built. Together, we've created something beautiful."

As the sun began to set, casting a warm glow over the festivities, Kurt took a moment to reflect on his journey. He had faced his past and emerged stronger, but more importantly, he had found a new family in the people of Kos. The shadows that had once haunted him were now replaced by the light of community and belonging.

As the evening continued, Kurt stood at the edge of the celebration, watching the villagers dance and laugh. He felt a deep sense of acceptance wash over him—acceptance of his past, of the battles fought, and of the life he had forged in the face of adversity.

In that moment, surrounded by the warmth of the community, Kurt knew he was finally home. The power of compounding wasn't just about tangible resources; it was about the connections formed and the love shared. He had learned that by investing in each other, they could create a future filled with hope and resilience.

With a renewed spirit, Kurt stepped into the heart of the festival, ready to embrace the joy of the moment. He had fought for this, and now he would cherish it. As laughter rang in the air and the stars twinkled overhead, Kurt felt at peace—finally free to embrace the life he had built on the island of Kos.

Chapter 14:

A New Beginning

As the festival drew to a close, the last remnants of daylight faded into twilight, leaving behind a tapestry of stars that blanketed the sky. The vibrant energy of the celebration lingered in the air, a testament to the unity and resilience of the community. Kurt felt a profound sense of satisfaction as he surveyed the scene—a scene filled with laughter, joy, and the promise of a brighter future.

After the last dance had been danced and the final song sung, the villagers began to disperse, each person carrying with them the warmth of the evening. Kurt lingered, his heart full as he helped clean up the remnants of the festivities. Eleni worked alongside him, her smile infectious as they gathered empty bottles and leftover food.

"You really did it, Kurt," she said, her eyes sparkling in the soft light. "This festival was a huge success."

Kurt shrugged, a modest grin on his face. "It was a team effort. Everyone played a part in making it happen."

Eleni paused for a moment, leaning against a stack of crates. "But you led us here. You brought everyone together and showed us that we could thrive, even in the face of adversity."

Her words resonated deeply within him. He had spent so long fighting battles alone, haunted by his past. Now, standing alongside Eleni and the villagers, he realized how far he had come. "I couldn't have done it without all of you. You've taught me the true meaning of community."

As they continued to clean up, the weight of the past began to lift even more. Kurt felt a sense of closure settling over him, as if the ghosts that had haunted him were finally fading into the distance. The shadows of regret were no longer a burden; instead, they had transformed into lessons that guided him forward.

When they finished tidying up, Kurt turned to Eleni, a newfound determination in his heart. "What do you think the future holds for us, for Kos?"

Eleni tilted her head, considering the question. "I think we can accomplish anything we set our minds to. We've built something beautiful here, and I believe it will only grow stronger."

Kurt nodded, feeling a surge of hope. "I want to be part of that growth. I want to help create a sustainable future for this island."

With a mischievous grin, Eleni replied, "Well, you're in luck. We have a lot of plans for the future. More community events, partnerships with local businesses, and even some eco-tourism initiatives."

"Eco-tourism?" Kurt raised an eyebrow, intrigued.

"Yes! We can showcase the beauty of Kos while preserving our environment," Eleni explained, her excitement palpable. "There's so much potential here."

Kurt felt the spark of inspiration ignite within him. "Let's start organizing workshops on sustainable practices. We can teach others how to protect our island while still enjoying its resources."

Eleni's eyes lit up. "That's a fantastic idea! We can gather experts to share their knowledge and empower the community."

As they discussed their ideas, Kurt felt a sense of purpose blossom within him. This was his new beginning—not just a continuation of his life on Kos, but a chance to build a legacy rooted in compassion, collaboration, and sustainability.

As they finished cleaning up and began to walk back toward the village, Kurt took a moment to absorb the beauty around him. The stars twinkled brightly overhead, a reminder of the vast possibilities that lay ahead. He felt a deep connection to the land, to the people, and to the life he had created on this island.

Arriving at the village square, they were met with the last few villagers sharing stories, the atmosphere still vibrant despite the late hour. Kurt and Eleni joined in, their spirits high as they recounted the highlights of the festival.

As laughter filled the air, Kurt felt a warmth in his heart. The community had not only overcome a significant threat but had also forged stronger bonds in the process. They had embraced their history, faced their fears, and emerged as a united front ready to take on the future.

Later that night, as Kurt prepared for bed, he reflected on his journey. The man who had arrived on Kos seeking solace had transformed into a protector, a leader, and a friend. He had found a home among the villagers, a place where he could contribute and belong.

With a sense of gratitude, he climbed into bed, the events of the day swirling in his mind. He closed his eyes, surrendering to the comforting embrace of sleep, knowing that a new dawn awaited him—a dawn filled with opportunities, challenges, and the promise of growth.

As the sun rose the next morning, Kurt awoke to the sound of birds singing outside his window. He stretched and took a moment to appreciate the peace that enveloped him. The weight of his past was still there, but it no longer defined him. He was ready to embrace this new beginning.

He dressed quickly and stepped outside, the fresh morning air invigorating him. As he made his way down the path toward the village, he felt a sense of purpose guiding him. He was determined to make the most of this opportunity, to help Kos flourish and to ensure that the bonds formed during their struggles would last.

As Kurt arrived at the village square, he was greeted by the sight of villagers bustling about, preparing for the day ahead. The atmosphere was filled with laughter and chatter, a testament to the resilience and unity they had built together.

With each step, Kurt felt the weight of responsibility settle on his shoulders. He was no longer just a solitary figure; he was part of something greater. Together, they would shape the future of Kos, turning their dreams into reality.

As he joined the villagers, sharing in their laughter and plans for the day, Kurt knew he had finally found his place. He was ready to embrace the challenges ahead, to fight for the future of the island, and to cherish the community that had become his family.

In that moment, Kurt understood the true power of compounding—not just in resources, but in relationships, resilience, and the unyielding spirit of a united community. He was ready to forge ahead, confident that they could weather any storm together.

With a renewed sense of purpose, Kurt stepped forward, ready to embrace the future.

Chapter 15:

A Shadow in the Distance

As the days turned into weeks, the village of Kos thrived. Kurt threw himself into the community initiatives, and with each passing day, he felt more rooted in the island's fabric. The festival had sparked a flame of collaboration, igniting a spirit of togetherness that had long been dormant. New workshops sprang up, teaching sustainable practices, and local businesses flourished as they attracted visitors eager to experience the island's charm.

But amid this newfound vitality, a sense of unease began to linger in the back of Kurt's mind. Though they had faced down Viktor and his associates, he couldn't shake the feeling that their victory was merely a temporary reprieve. The shadows of the past, though dimmed, had not entirely vanished.

One crisp morning, while working in the community garden, Kurt noticed a figure watching him from a distance. He squinted against the bright sun, trying to discern the silhouette against the backdrop of the vibrant greenery. As the figure drew closer, his heart raced with apprehension.

"Good morning!" Eleni called, approaching him with a basket of fresh vegetables. "What's got you so distracted?"

Kurt turned to her, his brow furrowed. "I thought I saw someone watching us."

Eleni glanced over her shoulder but saw only the tranquil surroundings. "Maybe it's just your imagination. We've all been on edge since the festival."

"Maybe," Kurt replied, still feeling the weight of uncertainty. "But I can't shake the feeling that we're not out of the woods yet."

They resumed their work, but Kurt kept a watchful eye on the perimeter of the garden. The vibrant colors of the flowers and vegetables provided a stark contrast to the dark thoughts swirling in his mind. He tried to focus on the task at hand, but the sense of unease lingered like a shadow at the edges of his thoughts.

That evening, as the sun dipped below the horizon, Kurt gathered with the villagers for a meeting at the taverna. They had decided to discuss the upcoming projects and ensure everyone was on the same page. As they settled in, Kurt noticed the atmosphere was a mix of excitement and apprehension, the previous days' hard work weighed against the uncertainty of the future.

Nikos stood at the front, addressing the group. "We've made incredible progress, but we must remain vigilant. The threats we faced may still linger. We need to be prepared for anything."

Kurt's heart raced as he listened to Nikos, echoing the concerns that had been nagging at him. "I agree. We've accomplished so much, but we can't let our guard down. We should consider setting up a watch or communication system in case anything seems off."

The villagers nodded in agreement, and the discussion shifted toward implementing a plan. They brainstormed ideas for maintaining safety while encouraging collaboration and support among the community.

As the meeting continued, Kurt noticed a flicker of movement at the window. He turned his head, and his heart dropped when he saw the figure again—standing just beyond the taverna, partially concealed by shadows. The unsettling feeling in his gut intensified.

"Excuse me for a moment," he said, rising abruptly from his seat.

Eleni caught his eye, concern etched on her face, but he knew he had to investigate. Stepping outside, Kurt squinted into the fading light, searching for the figure. The street was quiet, the only sound the soft rustling of leaves in the breeze.

"Hello?" Kurt called out, his voice steady. "Is someone there?"

Silence hung in the air, stretching out like a taut wire. Just as he began to think it was a trick of the light, a figure emerged from the shadows—a woman, cloaked in darkness.

"Who are you?" Kurt demanded, a mixture of caution and curiosity swirling within him.

The woman stepped forward, her face partially obscured by a hood. "I'm here to warn you, Kurt."

"Warn me about what?" he replied, keeping his distance. "Are you with Viktor?"

"No," she said, lowering her hood to reveal a striking face, her eyes piercing. "My name is

Sofia. I'm not your enemy. But Viktor is not done with you. He's been watching, planning his next move."

Kurt's heart raced, the tension in the air palpable. "How do you know this?"

"I have my sources," she replied, her voice calm but urgent. "Viktor is not the kind of man to walk away from defeat. He's regrouping, and he won't hesitate to come after you again."

Kurt's mind whirled, a sense of dread creeping in. "What does he want? We've made it clear that he's not welcome here."

Sofia stepped closer, her expression serious. "It's not just about revenge for him. It's about control. He wants the island and everything on it, including the resources and the people. You've become a symbol of resistance, and that makes you a target."

Kurt clenched his fists, anger flaring at the thought of Viktor's continued threats. "What can we do? We can't let him take what we've built."

Sofia took a deep breath, her eyes searching Kurt's. "You need to be prepared. Gather your allies, strengthen your defenses, and be ready for whatever he plans next. But also understand this—Viktor is cunning. He won't just come at you head-on; he'll look for weaknesses, for divisions within your community."

Kurt nodded, absorbing her words. "Thank you for the warning. But how can we trust you?"

Sofia's expression softened, a hint of vulnerability breaking through her steely demeanor. "I know what it's like to be trapped in someone else's game. I've seen what Viktor is capable of. I want to help you stop him, but you have to trust me."

Kurt hesitated, weighing his options. The stakes were too high to ignore, and he sensed a flicker of sincerity in Sofia's voice. "All right. But we'll be cautious. I'll need to speak with my friends."

As they walked back toward the taverna, Kurt's mind raced with possibilities. This new alliance could provide the insight and support they needed to counter Viktor's plans, but he was aware of the risks involved.

Once inside, he turned to the villagers, who had noticed his absence. "We have a situation," he said, drawing their attention. "I just spoke with someone who claims to have information about Viktor. Her name is Sofia, and she says he's planning his next move against us."

Murmurs of concern rippled through the group. Kurt gestured for them to quiet down. "She's offered to help us, but we need to decide as a community how to proceed."

Nikos stepped forward, his brow furrowed. "We need to be careful. If she's associated with Viktor, we can't trust her."

Kurt shook his head. "I understand the hesitation, but if what she says is true, we need all the help we can get. We can't let fear dictate our actions. We've faced Viktor before, and we can do it again."

The villagers exchanged glances, their expressions a mixture of uncertainty and resolve. Finally, Eleni spoke up. "If Kurt believes in her, then we should at least hear her out. We can gather information and take precautions at the same time."

With the group's agreement, Kurt turned to Sofia, who stood silently at the back of the room, watching the dynamics unfold. "We'd like to hear more about what you know."

Sofia nodded, her expression serious. "I'll share everything I can. But first, we need to get you organized. If we're going to counter Viktor's plans, we'll need a solid strategy."

As they delved into discussions about their defenses and potential tactics, Kurt felt a renewed sense of determination. With Sofia's insights and the strength of the community behind him, they stood a better chance of facing whatever Viktor had in store.

The shadows of the past still lingered, but for the first time in a long time, Kurt felt ready to confront them. He wasn't just fighting for himself; he was fighting for his home and the people who had become his family. Together, they would face whatever challenges lay ahead.

Chapter 16:

Fortifying the Defences

The atmosphere in the taverna was electric as Kurt and the villagers gathered around a makeshift table to strategize against Viktor's potential return. With Sofia now included in their plans, her insights proved invaluable, shedding light on Viktor's methods and operations.

"First, we need to understand how he operates," Sofia began, her tone serious as she laid out a map of the island on the table. "Viktor is strategic; he'll try to exploit any weaknesses he can find. We have to anticipate his moves."

Kurt leaned in, studying the map closely. "What do you suggest we focus on first?"

Sofia pointed to various locations. "These are the main entry points to the island—ports, narrow passages, and popular tourist spots. We need to fortify these areas and establish lookout points to monitor any unusual activity."

Nikos nodded, his expression determined. "We can organize patrols around the harbor and the village. The more eyes we have, the better prepared we'll be."

Kurt felt a surge of hope. "We can also set up community watch groups. If everyone is involved, we can ensure that we're all looking out for each other."

As they discussed potential defenses, the villagers became increasingly animated. Ideas flowed, each person contributing their unique perspectives and skills. They brainstormed ways to secure their homes, reinforce the village boundaries, and communicate effectively in case of an emergency.

Hours passed as they worked through the details, and by the end of the meeting, a comprehensive plan had begun to take shape. The villagers felt empowered, united in their mission to protect their home.

As the sun began to set, casting a warm glow over the taverna, Kurt felt a deep sense of pride. They had come together in a way he had never imagined possible.

"Let's meet again tomorrow morning to finalize our plans and assign roles," he said, his voice filled with encouragement. "Together, we can face whatever Viktor throws at us."

The villagers cheered, their spirits high as they left the taverna, motivated by the knowledge that they were taking action to secure their future.

After everyone had dispersed, Kurt found himself lingering in the quiet of the taverna. Sofia was still there, organizing her notes and gathering her thoughts.

"Thank you for trusting me," she said, glancing up from the table. "I know I'm still an outsider, but I want to help."

Kurt nodded, appreciating her sincerity. "You've proven your worth. Your knowledge is invaluable to us. I just hope we can outsmart Viktor."

Sofia's expression turned serious. "Viktor is dangerous, Kurt. He won't give up easily. We need to be ready for anything."

Kurt met her gaze, determination settling in. "We will be. I won't let him threaten this community again."

Over the next few days, preparations intensified. The villagers banded together, working tirelessly to implement their defense strategies. They set up lookout posts around the village, reinforcing the main entrance with barricades and ensuring that each person understood their role in the community watch.

Kurt felt a renewed sense of purpose as he took on the responsibility of training the villagers in self-defense techniques. He wanted them to feel empowered, capable of standing their ground if necessary. Eleni joined him, her enthusiasm infectious as they worked together to build the villagers' confidence.

"Remember," Kurt instructed as they practiced, "the goal isn't just to fight; it's to protect and to escape if you need to. Use your surroundings to your advantage."

The villagers absorbed the lessons, and Kurt could see their fear transforming into determination. Each session brought them closer together, strengthening their resolve and deepening their connections.

However, as the days wore on, Kurt couldn't shake the feeling that time was running out.

Viktor was out there, plotting his next move, and Kurt had to be ready for whatever came next.

One evening, after a long day of training, Kurt returned to his cottage, exhausted but satisfied. He poured himself a glass of water and stepped outside, feeling the cool breeze against his skin. The stars sparkled overhead, a reminder of the vastness of the world beyond the island.

As he stood there, he heard the soft sound of footsteps approaching. Turning, he saw Eleni walking toward him, her expression thoughtful.

"Hey," she said softly. "I thought I'd find you here."

Kurt smiled, his heart warming at her presence. "Just taking a moment to reflect. We've made great progress, but I can't shake this feeling of unease."

Eleni stepped closer, her eyes searching his. "I understand. But we're stronger now. We've built something together, and we can't let Viktor take that away from us."

"You're right," Kurt replied, appreciating her unwavering support. "I just wish I knew what he was planning. It would make it easier to prepare."

"Maybe we should try to find out," she suggested, a glint of mischief in her eyes. "If we can gather information about his movements, we could anticipate his next steps."

Kurt's mind raced with possibilities. "You're right. If we can infiltrate his operation again, we might discover more about his plans."

Eleni grinned. "Let's gather a small group of the villagers who can help us. We'll need to be careful, but if we can get close, we might be able to learn something crucial."

As they discussed their plan, Kurt felt a spark of hope ignite within him. They had faced Viktor before, and they could do it again. With the support of the community behind them, they had the potential to turn the tide.

The next day, Kurt and Eleni gathered a small group of villagers—those who had shown interest in the previous infiltration. They discussed the plan, outlining their goals and the importance of discretion.

"Remember," Kurt said, looking each person in the eye, "our primary objective is to gather information. We cannot let ourselves be seen or draw attention to our actions."

As they made their preparations, the villagers felt a renewed sense of purpose. They knew they were fighting for their home and their future, and that was worth every risk.

As they set off toward the old hotel where Viktor had been spotted, Kurt felt a sense of determination wash over him. He wasn't just reclaiming his life; he was fighting for the very essence of the community that had welcomed him.

With every step they took, Kurt felt the shadows of the past receding. He was ready to confront whatever lay ahead, knowing that the bonds forged through struggle and collaboration would guide him through.

As they approached the hotel, the atmosphere shifted. The weight of anticipation settled over the group as they prepared to face the unknown. This time, they would not be caught off guard.

Together, they would uncover the truth and fortify their defenses against the threat that loomed in the distance.

Chapter 17:

Into the Lion's Den

The moon hung high in the sky, casting an ethereal glow over the old hotel as Kurt and the small group of villagers approached. The building loomed before them, a relic of a bygone era, now shadowed by uncertainty and danger. Kurt felt the weight of the moment settle on his shoulders; this was the heart of Viktor's operations, and they were stepping into the lion's den.

"Stay close and keep your voices down," Kurt whispered, his heart racing with adrenaline. The group nodded in acknowledgment, each person feeling the gravity of the situation.

They moved stealthily around the perimeter of the hotel, their senses heightened. Kurt led the way, recalling the layout from his previous visit, and he gestured for the others to pause at a side entrance that led to the back of the building.

"This way," he instructed, slipping through the door with caution. Inside, the air was stale, the remnants of past gatherings lingering like ghosts. The dim light from flickering bulbs cast unsettling shadows along the walls.

As they crept through the corridor, Kurt's mind raced with the potential dangers that lay ahead. "Remember, our goal is to gather information," he reiterated. "If we see Viktor or his men, we'll retreat and regroup."

Eleni stayed close, her presence a steadying force amidst the uncertainty. "We can do this," she whispered, her determination shining through.

They moved quietly, listening for any sounds of activity. Kurt's heart pounded in his chest as they reached a doorway that led into the main lobby. Peeking through the crack, he saw several of Viktor's associates gathered around a table, their voices low but urgent.

Kurt motioned for the group to huddle closer, their breaths held as they strained to hear.

"We need to finalize the logistics for the shipment," one of the men said, his tone serious. "Viktor wants to ensure everything goes smoothly this time."

Kurt exchanged glances with Eleni, a sense of urgency washing over him. "We have to find out what they're planning. We can't let them take control of the island."

Eleni nodded, her eyes reflecting the determination that had drawn them all together. "Let's get closer."

Carefully, they maneuvered around the edges of the lobby, staying hidden behind furniture and shadows. Kurt's pulse quickened as he strained to hear more of the conversation.

"They've been getting too bold," another man added. "The locals are starting to catch on. We need to send a message."

Kurt's stomach churned at the implications of their words. Viktor's plans were more sinister than he had anticipated, and they needed to act quickly to disrupt whatever was in motion.

"Look," Kurt whispered to the group, pointing to a door at the far end of the lobby. "If we can slip into the back office, we might find more information about their operations."

The group nodded, their resolve strengthened by the urgency of the situation. They moved toward the door, staying low and silent. As they approached, Kurt could hear the muffled voices behind him growing louder, and he felt the weight of the moment pressing down on him.

He reached for the doorknob, his heart racing as he turned it slowly. The door creaked open, revealing a dimly lit office cluttered with papers and maps. Kurt stepped inside, followed by the others, closing the door quietly behind them.

The room smelled of dust and old wood, and the flickering light from a small lamp illuminated the scattered documents. Kurt quickly scanned the space, his eyes landing on a large map spread across the desk, covered in markings and notes.

"This must be it," he said, moving closer to the desk. "We can find out exactly what they're planning."

As the group gathered around, Kurt leaned over the map, his fingers tracing the routes and locations marked with red ink. "These are transport routes, probably for their shipments. If we can gather this information and get it back to the villagers, we can formulate a plan to counteract their operations."

Eleni leaned closer, her brow furrowed in concentration. "Look here—this location," she said, pointing to a marked spot on the map. "It's near the old harbor. If they're planning to move shipments there, we need to warn the others."

Suddenly, a noise from outside the office made them freeze. Kurt's heart raced as he strained to listen. The door rattled slightly, and they exchanged worried glances. They couldn't afford to be caught now.

"Hide!" Kurt hissed, and the group scattered, ducking behind furniture and stacks of boxes as the door opened.

Viktor's voice cut through the air, sharp and commanding. "We need to discuss our next steps. If we're going to move forward, I can't have any distractions."

Kurt held his breath, the tension thick in the air as he tried to remain hidden. He could see Viktor entering the office, flanked by two of his associates. They moved closer to the desk, and Kurt's heart sank as he realized they were right beside the map.

"Check those shipments again. We can't afford any mistakes this time," Viktor said, his voice low but filled with authority. "The locals are getting too curious. We need to act quickly."

Kurt felt anger simmering beneath the surface, but he knew he had to remain calm. They needed to gather as much information as possible without being detected.

Viktor continued to speak, his words heavy with menace. "If anyone gets in our way, we'll handle them decisively. I won't allow anyone to disrupt our plans again."

Kurt exchanged a glance with Eleni, whose expression mirrored his concern. They needed to act before it was too late.

With a deep breath, Kurt signaled to the others to prepare for their exit. He would have to confront Viktor directly, but they needed to get back to the safety of the village first.

"On my mark," he whispered, readying himself for action.

Viktor and his associates continued to discuss logistics, unaware of the presence lurking just beyond their sight. The moment felt electric, tension hanging thick in the air as Kurt prepared for the final push.

"Now!" Kurt commanded, bursting from his hiding spot and lunging toward Viktor. The element of surprise was their greatest weapon, and he was determined to seize it.

"Get back!" Viktor shouted, drawing a weapon from his side as Kurt charged.

But before he could react, Kurt tackled him, sending the both of them crashing to the ground. The room erupted into chaos as the two associates lunged forward, but the villagers emerged from their hiding places, tackling the remaining men and wrestling for control.

Eleni fought beside Kurt, her determination unyielding as they grappled with Viktor. "We can't let him escape!" she shouted, her voice fierce and resolute.

Kurt felt the adrenaline surge through him, focusing all his energy on subduing Viktor. The fight was intense, filled with grunts and shouts, but Kurt knew they had to contain him.

Finally, with a swift maneuver, Kurt pinned Viktor's arms to the ground, his heart racing. "This ends now, Viktor! You're not going to threaten our community again!"

Viktor struggled beneath him, anger and desperation flashing in his eyes. "You think this is over? You don't understand what you're up against!"

"We understand perfectly," Kurt replied, his voice steady. "You've underestimated us, and it's going to cost you."

Just then, one of the associates broke free and charged toward Kurt, but Eleni intercepted him, delivering a swift kick that sent him sprawling back against the desk.

"Stay down!" she shouted, eyes blazing with determination.

As Kurt continued to hold Viktor down, he felt the weight of the moment settle around him. They were finally facing their enemy, and it was a culmination of everything he had fought for—a chance to protect the island and its people once and for all.

"Call the others!" Kurt shouted to the villagers. "We need to secure him!"

One of the locals rushed to the door, ready to summon reinforcements. The tide had turned, and Viktor's reign of intimidation was coming to an end.

"Your time is up, Viktor," Kurt said, his voice low but filled with authority. "You've lost."

As the commotion continued, Kurt felt a sense of clarity. The past had haunted him for far too long, but now he was reclaiming his life—not just for himself, but for the island and the community that had embraced him.

With every ounce of strength, he held Viktor down, refusing to let go until they had secured their victory. The shadows of the past were finally beginning to dissipate, replaced by the hope of a brighter future.

Chapter 18:

The Final Stand

The air was thick with tension as Kurt held Viktor pinned to the ground, the chaos of the struggle swirling around them. The villagers were working together, subduing Viktor's associates and reclaiming control of the situation. Each moment felt charged with the energy of a battle fought for their future.

"Get the ropes!" Kurt shouted to the villagers. "We need to secure him before he has a chance to escape!"

As one of the locals dashed to retrieve some sturdy ropes from the storage closet, Kurt maintained his grip on Viktor, who squirmed beneath him, a mix of fury and desperation etched on his face.

"You think this will stop me? I will always find a way to come back!" Viktor spat, venom dripping from his words.

Kurt leaned closer, his voice low and steady. "Not this time. You've underestimated us for the last time. Kos will not fall under your control."

The villagers returned, quickly binding Viktor's wrists and ankles. With each knot tightened, Kurt felt a surge of satisfaction. They were reclaiming their home, and the power dynamics were shifting in their favor.

"Is everyone okay?" Eleni called out as she helped to subdue one of Viktor's associates. The villagers nodded, breathing heavily but determined. The adrenaline of the moment fueled their resolve.

"Secure the entrances!" Kurt ordered. "We can't let any of them escape or call for reinforcements."

As the locals moved to fortify the hotel's exits, Kurt focused on Viktor, whose defiance only seemed to grow. "You may have won this round, but you will regret this, Kurt. You have no idea who you're dealing with," Viktor warned, his eyes glinting with malice.

Kurt's heart raced, but he refused to show fear. "I know exactly who you are—a coward hiding behind intimidation. Your reign of terror ends tonight."

As the final knots were secured, Kurt stood back, breathing heavily. The room felt charged with energy, the weight of the confrontation lingering in the air. Viktor glared at him, defiance flickering in his gaze.

"Where are your allies, Viktor? Are they going to come rescue you?" Kurt taunted, wanting to provoke a response.

Viktor chuckled darkly, the sound echoing off the walls. "They're not coming for me. They'll come for you. You've made a powerful enemy tonight."

Kurt shook his head, feeling the confidence of the villagers around him. "No, we're standing together. We're not afraid of you or your threats anymore."

Just then, the door burst open, and more locals entered, armed with makeshift weapons and fierce determination. The sight of reinforcements brought a renewed sense of energy to the room, and Kurt felt a sense of camaraderie enveloping him.

"We heard the commotion!" one of the newcomers shouted, eyes scanning the scene. "What do you need?"

Kurt stepped forward, feeling the solidarity of the group behind him. "We have Viktor and his associates contained. Let's ensure they can't get out or call for help. We'll need to discuss our next steps."

As they secured the remaining associates, the atmosphere shifted from one of fear to empowerment. Kurt took a moment to breathe deeply, feeling the collective strength of the villagers solidifying around him. This was their stand against tyranny, their declaration of independence.

Once everyone was contained, Kurt turned to Viktor, whose expression shifted from anger to frustration. "You're making a mistake. You think you can control everything, but you're just delaying the inevitable."

Kurt stepped closer, unwavering. "The only mistake here was underestimating us. Kos is a community, and we fight for each other. You've lost your power over us."

Viktor's eyes narrowed, calculating. "You'll regret this, Kurt. You'll pay for your defiance."

The tension in the room was palpable, but Kurt felt a surge of resolve. "No more threats. No more fear. This ends here."

As they secured Viktor and his associates, Kurt gathered the villagers to discuss their next steps. The battle had shifted in their favor, but he knew they needed to strategize carefully to ensure their safety.

"We need to decide what to do with them," Kurt said, looking around the group. "We can't let them go; they will come back, and we need to make sure we send a clear message."

Nikos stepped forward, his expression grave. "We should turn them over to the authorities. Let them face justice for what they've done."

"But what if they escape?" another villager countered, concern etched on their face. "What if Viktor has connections that can help him?"

Kurt nodded, considering the implications. "We can't let our guard down. Whatever we decide, we need to ensure that they can't threaten us again."

As the discussions continued, Kurt felt the weight of leadership settle upon him. He had fought for this community, and now he had to guide them through this next phase. They had come too far to let fear dictate their future.

Finally, they reached a consensus. They would secure Viktor and his associates in the hotel until they could arrange for their transfer to the authorities. The villagers would rotate shifts, keeping watch over them until help arrived.

As they moved to reinforce the hotel's defenses, Kurt felt a sense of camaraderie solidifying among the group. They had faced a formidable threat and emerged stronger, united in purpose.

Later that night, as the moon cast a silvery light over the island, Kurt found a moment of solitude to reflect on the events that had unfolded. He stood on the terrace, looking out at the sea, the calm waves a stark contrast to the storm they had just weathered.

The shadows of his past still lingered, but they no longer felt like a burden. Instead, they were a part of his journey—a reminder of how far he had come and the strength he had found within himself and the community.

With each passing moment, he felt more connected to Kos, to the people who had embraced him as one of their own. He had fought for their future, and in doing so, he had discovered a new sense of purpose.

As Kurt prepared for bed, a newfound peace settled over him. He was ready for whatever challenges lay ahead, determined to protect the island and its people. They had faced down Viktor, but the fight was not yet over. Together, they would fortify their defenses and stand firm against any threat, ready to embrace the dawn of a new day.

Chapter 19:

Shadows of the Past

The days following the confrontation with Viktor and his associates passed in a blur of activity. The village was abuzz with preparations, and Kurt felt the weight of responsibility as he worked alongside the locals to fortify their defenses. They had successfully contained Viktor, but the reality of their situation still loomed large—his influence and connections would not disappear easily.

Kurt spent hours planning and coordinating with the villagers, each meeting reinforcing the bonds they had forged. But as much as he immersed himself in the present, the shadows of his past continued to flicker at the edges of his consciousness.

One evening, while walking along the beach to clear his mind, Kurt found himself reflecting on his years in the SAS. The memories came rushing back—faces of comrades lost, decisions that haunted him, and battles fought in distant lands. The weight of it all pressed down on him like a heavy cloak.

Sitting on the sand, Kurt stared out at the horizon, the waves crashing rhythmically against the shore. It was a soothing sound, but it couldn't drown out the memories that resurfaced unbidden.

"Why did I choose this life?" he muttered to himself, frustration bubbling to the surface. He had sought solace on Kos, hoping to escape the ghosts of his past, but they followed him relentlessly.

As he sat lost in thought, he became aware of a presence beside him. Turning, he saw Eleni approaching, concern etched on her features.

"Kurt," she said softly, taking a seat beside him. "I thought I'd find you here. Are you okay?"

Kurt hesitated, unsure of how to voice the turmoil within him. "Just thinking about everything that's happened. It's been a lot."

Eleni nodded, her expression empathetic. "It has been. But you've handled it all with such strength. You've brought us together and helped us reclaim our home."

"I appreciate that, but sometimes it feels like the past is always lurking just out of sight," Kurt confessed, his voice heavy. "I can't shake the memories of what I've done, the people I've lost. I thought coming here would help me find peace, but it seems like the shadows still follow me."

Eleni reached out, placing a reassuring hand on his arm. "You're not defined by your past, Kurt. You've fought for a new beginning here, for the people of Kos. That's what matters."

Her words resonated with him, yet doubt lingered in the recesses of his mind. "I just don't know if I can escape it completely. Every time I close my eyes, I see the faces of those who didn't make it back."

Eleni's expression softened, her gaze unwavering. "You're not alone in this. We all carry our burdens, but together, we can find a way to heal. You've built something meaningful here. It's never too late to let go of the pain."

As Kurt absorbed her words, he felt a flicker of hope ignite within him. Perhaps this was a chance to redefine himself, to turn his pain into purpose. He had spent so long running from the shadows; maybe it was time to confront them.

"Thank you, Eleni," he said, his voice steadying. "I need to find a way to honor those I've lost, to channel this pain into something positive."

"Then let's do it together," she suggested. "We can create a memorial, a space where people can remember those who have sacrificed for the greater good. It can be a place of healing for everyone in the village."

Kurt's heart swelled at the idea. "A memorial would be a way to remember them and acknowledge their sacrifices. It could also serve as a reminder of why we fight for this community."

Eleni smiled, her enthusiasm infectious. "Yes! We can involve everyone—share stories, create a space where people can come together and reflect. It will help us heal as a community."

As they sat on the beach, their conversation flowed, filled with hope and determination. The idea of a memorial sparked a new purpose within Kurt, a way to honor the past while embracing the future.

In the following days, Kurt and Eleni gathered the villagers to discuss their plans. The response was overwhelmingly positive, with everyone eager to contribute. They began brainstorming ideas for the memorial, sharing stories and memories of those they had lost.

As the villagers worked together, Kurt felt the weight of his past slowly begin to lift. Each story shared, each contribution made, was a step toward healing—not just for him but for the entire community.

They decided to build the memorial at the edge of the village, overlooking the sea—a place where the waves could wash over the stones, a reminder of the lives lost and the hope that remained. The villagers collected stones, each one representing a story, a life, a sacrifice.

As the days turned into weeks, the memorial began to take shape. Kurt poured his heart into the project, each stone laid a tribute to the comrades he had lost and a symbol of the resilience of the community.

On the day of the unveiling, the atmosphere was somber yet hopeful. Villagers gathered, their faces reflecting the weight of the moment. Kurt stood before them, Eleni by his side, as they prepared to share the significance of the memorial.

"Today, we gather to honor those we have lost," Kurt began, his voice steady but filled with emotion. "Each stone here represents a life, a sacrifice made in the pursuit of something greater. They fought for freedom, for peace, and for the values we hold dear."

Tears glistened in the eyes of the villagers, and a sense of unity enveloped them. "Let this memorial serve as a reminder of our strength, our resilience, and our commitment to one another. We honor their memories by standing together, by protecting this community, and by embracing the future."

As Kurt finished speaking, he felt a wave of catharsis wash over him. The shadows that had once haunted him began to fade, replaced by a sense of acceptance and peace. He was no longer defined by his past; he was part of something greater—a community that stood united against adversity.

The villagers stepped forward, placing flowers and stones at the base of the memorial. Each act was a tribute, a commitment to remember those who had paved the way for their freedom.

As the sun dipped below the horizon, casting a golden glow over the memorial, Kurt felt a profound sense of gratitude. He had come to Kos seeking solace, but he had found a family—a community that had embraced him and fought alongside him.

In that moment, surrounded by the love and support of his friends, Kurt knew he was ready to face whatever challenges lay ahead. The shadows of the past may linger, but they would no longer hold power over him. He had reclaimed his life, his purpose, and the promise of a brighter future.

As the villagers celebrated their resilience and commitment, Kurt felt a sense of belonging wash over him. Together, they had turned pain into purpose, forging a new beginning rooted in hope, strength, and unity.

Chapter 20:

A New Dawn

The days following the unveiling of the memorial were filled with a renewed sense of purpose on Kos. The community had come together to honor their past, but more importantly, they had embraced their future. The memorial stood as a beacon of resilience, a testament to the strength of the bonds they had forged.

As the sun rose over the horizon, bathing the village in a warm golden light, Kurt felt a sense of hope and renewal. The island had transformed, both in spirit and in its community. Each day brought new opportunities to grow, to learn, and to thrive.

Kurt awoke early, the sound of birds chirping outside his window inviting him to greet the day. After a quick breakfast, he set out toward the village square, eager to see what the day would bring. The air was crisp and invigorating, filling him with energy as he walked the familiar path.

When he arrived, he found the villagers bustling about, preparing for the day's activities. Children laughed and played in the streets, their joy infectious. Kurt smiled, feeling a warmth spread through him at the sight of the thriving community.

"Good morning, Kurt!" a neighbor called, waving as he passed. "Are you ready for the fishing competition today?"

Kurt chuckled, recalling how the villagers had decided to organize a friendly fishing competition as a way to promote camaraderie and showcase their skills. "I'm ready! I just hope I can keep up with all of you!"

Eleni joined him, a radiant smile on her face. "You'll do great. Just remember what we practiced about using your surroundings to your advantage!"

They shared a laugh, and Kurt felt a sense of ease settle over him. He had come to appreciate the simple joys of life on Kos—the laughter, the friendships, and the sense of belonging that had eluded him for so long.

As the competition kicked off, the villagers gathered at the harbor, excitement palpable in the air. The water sparkled under the sun, a beautiful blue canvas waiting to be filled with the day's adventures. Kurt joined the others as they prepared their boats and gear, ready to embrace the friendly rivalry.

"Remember, it's not just about catching the biggest fish; it's about enjoying the time together," Kurt reminded the group as they gathered.

As the competition began, laughter filled the air, and the sound of splashing water accompanied their friendly banter. Kurt felt alive, surrounded by friends who had become family. Each cast of the line was a reminder of the bonds they had forged through shared struggles and triumphs.

Hours passed as they competed, the atmosphere filled with joy and camaraderie. Kurt caught a few fish, but it was the laughter and connections that made the day truly special. As the sun began to set, painting the sky in hues of orange and pink, they gathered on the shore to celebrate their successes, big and small.

Nikos stood at the forefront, holding a trophy—a simple but heartfelt gesture to honor the winner of the day's competition. "And the winner is…" he began, a smile spreading across his face as he announced the victor. "Kurt!"

The crowd erupted into cheers, and Kurt felt a mix of pride and humility. "Thank you! But this is a victory for all of us. We've worked hard together, and today was a reminder of what we can achieve as a community."

As they shared stories and laughter around a bonfire, Kurt took a moment to reflect on how far they had come. The shadows of his past had been transformed into a foundation of strength, guiding him toward a brighter future.

As the night wore on and the stars twinkled above, Kurt felt a deep sense of contentment. He had faced his demons, embraced the love of his newfound family, and found a sense of belonging he had long thought lost.

"Here's to the future of Kos!" Eleni raised her cup, her eyes sparkling with enthusiasm.

"Here's to us!" Kurt echoed, the warmth of community wrapping around him like a comforting blanket.

As they clinked their cups together, Kurt felt a renewed sense of hope—a belief that together, they could face whatever challenges lay ahead. The memories of the past would always be a part of him, but they no longer defined him.

In that moment, surrounded by laughter, friendship, and the promise of new beginnings, Kurt realized that he had found his true home. Kos was not just an island; it was a community built on resilience, love, and the strength to stand united.

As the fire crackled and the stars shone brightly above, Kurt knew that this was just the beginning. Together, they would continue to nurture their bonds, celebrate their victories, and face any challenges that came their way. The dawn of a new chapter awaited them, filled with endless possibilities.

With a heart full of hope and a spirit ready for the adventures ahead, Kurt embraced the future—no longer haunted by the past, but inspired by the journey they had shared.

Epilogue: Whispers of Change

Months passed since the fishing competition that had solidified Kurt's place within the community of Kos. The memorial stood proudly at the edge of the village, a testament to resilience and the lives that had shaped their future. The villagers worked tirelessly to preserve their traditions while embracing sustainable practices that ensured the island thrived.

Yet, as Kurt settled into his new life, he couldn't shake the feeling that change was on the horizon. Whispers of unrest had begun to circulate among the villagers. Rumors of Viktor's return—of his relentless pursuit of power—were becoming more than just idle chatter. The shadows that had briefly retreated were starting to gather once more.

One evening, as the sun dipped low on the horizon, casting a golden hue over the island, Kurt gathered with Eleni and Nikos at the taverna. The atmosphere was charged, a sense of unease settling over their discussions.

"We've been hearing reports of strange ships off the coast," Nikos said, his brow furrowed. "They don't belong to anyone we know."

Kurt leaned forward, concern etching his features. "Viktor could be trying to establish new routes for his operations. If he's back, we need to be prepared."

Eleni nodded, her expression serious. "We can't let him undermine everything we've built. We need to increase our watch and gather more information about what's happening."

As they strategized, a sense of urgency enveloped the room. They couldn't afford to ignore the signs. The hard-won peace they had fought for was fragile, and the threat of Viktor's return loomed like a dark cloud on the horizon.

Days later, as the villagers worked together to fortify their defenses, a small fishing boat approached the shore. Kurt's heart raced as he recognized the familiar silhouette—it was Sofia. She had been gathering intel, but her unexpected arrival ignited a flicker of hope amidst the growing tension.

"Something is happening," Sofia said breathlessly as she stepped onto the beach. "Viktor is not just planning a return; he's forming alliances with other groups, dangerous ones. He intends to take back what he believes is his."

Kurt exchanged worried glances with Eleni and Nikos. "We need to know what we're up against," he said, determination rising within him. "We've faced him once, but if he's gathering forces, we have to be ready for a fight."

Sofia nodded, her gaze steady. "I have contacts on the mainland. We can gather information and potentially find allies who understand what's at stake."

As they stood together, the winds of change swept through the island, and Kurt felt a sense of purpose ignite within him. He would not let Viktor destroy the life he had fought to build. The community he had come to cherish was worth every effort, every sacrifice.

Kurt looked out at the shimmering sea, feeling the weight of the moment settle around him. "Then let's do it. We'll gather our allies, strengthen our defenses, and prepare for whatever comes next. Kos is our home, and we will protect it."

As the sun set on the horizon, casting an orange glow over the island, Kurt knew that a new chapter awaited them. The fight was far from over, but he felt ready to embrace the challenges ahead. United with his community and fueled by their shared determination, Kurt was prepared to confront the shadows that threatened their future.

With a renewed sense of purpose, they set out to face the challenges that lay ahead. The battle for Kos had just begun, and Kurt would fight not just for the island but for the bonds of friendship and love that had anchored him to this place.

Together, they would forge a path forward, transforming fear into strength and uncertainty into resolve. The whispers of change were just the beginning, and Kurt was ready to stand firm against the coming storm.

Books by Karl Hartey to check out

Financial & Personal Development Books
Smart Money Series

1. **Smart Money: How to Create Financial Freedom**
2. **Smart Money: Retirement Made Simple**
3. **Smart Money: Securing Your Legacy**
4. **Smart Money: Tax Efficiency for High Earners**
5. **Smart Money: Investing with Confidence**

Other Financial Books

6. **How to Survive the Sharks** – Insider knowledge on the financial services industry.
7. **All You Need to Know About Retirement** – Insights into retirement and pension planning.
8. **All You Need to Know About Divorce and Financial Settlements** – Navigating divorce and financial settlements.
9. **All You Need to Know About Trusts** – Understanding the role and use of trusts.
10. **All You Need to Know About Investing** – A guide to understanding investments.
11. **Securing Your Family's Financial Future: 60 Top Tips** – Practical advice for financial security.

12. **All You Need to Know About Inheritance Tax and Estate Planning** – Resourceful guide on estate planning and tax.

Gumball Rally Adventures

1. **3000 Miles: Our First Gumball Rally**
2. **Gumball 3000: Miami to Ibiza**
3. **Gumball 3000: Dublin to Bucharest**
4. **Gumball 3000: Riga to Mykonos**

Mollie and Tobie Series

Cornish Tails Series

1. **Mollie and Tobie: Cornish Tails**
2. **Mollie and Tobie: Cornish Tails 2**
3. **Mollie and Tobie: Cornish Tails 3**
4. **Mollie and Tobie: Cornish Tails 4**
5. **Mollie and Tobie: Cornish Tails 5** (Famous Dog Walks in Cornwall)

Other Adventures

6. **Mollie and Tobie: Greek Tails**
7. **Mollie and Tobie: Shropshire Tails**
8. **Mollie and Tobie: Cheshire Tails**
9. **Mollie and Tobie: The Wrexham Wolfpack**
10. **Mollie and Tobie: Dubai Adventures**

Mysteries and Sci-Fi

Seasonal Nature Walks Series

Animated Stories in Progress

Printed in Great Britain
by Amazon

57500722R00106